Satyameva Jayate

Satyameva Jayate

Vadassery Thaiparambil Rakesh

First self-published in India 2018 by
Vadassery Thaiparambil Rakesh
205, Panchmukhi Apartment,
Opp: Nutan School,
Newsama Road,
Vadodara, Gujarat- 390024
India
Email: vtrakesh@hotmail.com
https://authorrakesh.wordpress.com
https://www.facebook.com/vtrakesh/

Book Edition: 1

About the Author

V.T.Rakesh is a crime-thriller writer based out of Surat, India. His debut book 'The Thorough Check', published in 2013, was critically acclaimed and reviewed by many including 'The Tribune'. It was featured in 'Krithi', literature festival held in Kochi on 10th March 2018. His second book 'Deliverance of Sarpameru', published in 2015, was about a deluge and the subsequent relief activities, which brought three warring communities together. 'Carpathian Cantos', a collection of poems published in July 2018, shows the softer side of this fiction writer. 'Satyameva Jayate' is his third book in the genre of crime-thrillers.

Acknowledgements

This is my third book in this genre. I am short of words to thank my wife and son, for having sacrificed their weekend outings for me to complete these three books. I am indebted to my parents and also my in-laws for the blessings showered on me. No words are enough to thank my editor Ms Nikita Jhanglani, who has really transformed this book.

Dedication

Dedicated to my dear wife, Nisha

Chapter 1

That night, Bala had hit the sack very early. Next morning, he had to rush to the neighbouring convent school to buy admission forms for his daughter. The school was a coveted school, and it was a dream for any salaried-class person to get his child into it. Bala but was very much confident about his brilliant daughter who always stood first in her present school. The queue to the purchase of forms started at 5.00 in the morning.

It took more than a dozen rings of the telephone for Bala to wake up from his deep slumber. And it took that many seconds for him to figure out that he was supposed to answer the phone which was continuously ringing as if it was an emergency. He looked at the clock and it was ten minutes past midnight. The name of Sudarshanam was popping out of the brand-new Nokia mobile set's screen, as if in case he did not take the phone, the person would physically pop out and catch the neck of Bala. Then again, given the reputation of Sudarshanam, the Nokia phone was very much giving the right impression.

Sudarshanam was a terror among the junior colleagues. Especially after he gets drunk. He had a penchant for 'Black Dog' whiskey, which he guzzled down every night. And it was his routine to call his juniors to do performance reviews during these nights. There were cases of slapping, fainting and even people absconding from employment after that. The disgruntled juniors started calling him the colloquial translation of 'Black Dog', *Kaala Kutta*, which subsequently got abbreviated to KK.

Hence when Bala saw that name flashing on the screen, he smelled disaster and in no time, sleepiness vanished from his face. He looked at the innocent faces of his wife and daughter blissfully immersed in deep slumber. He inched his way silently outside into the balcony without disturbing their sleep.

"Why are you taking so much time to lift the call?" KK roared from the other end. Bala had wetted the underwear already. "Sirrrr, I was in the toilet." answered a fumbling Bala. "You don't even wait to wash your arse, just come down in your lungi, start your car and reach the Monarch bar in ten minutes." KK slammed the phone.

Bala was in a dilemma. If he goes to the bar, KK will not spare him for the night. More than the ragging and the ordeal, what bothered him was that coveted admission which he may miss for his only child. He glimpsed through the curtains, he could see the lovely and peaceful face of his sleeping daughter, may be dreaming about her new school. The phone call had woken up his wife Saroja, and she came out like a cat, lest they wake up the child. They talked mainly through animations, and finally going by Saroja's actions it was evident she gave him a strict red signal to go, and left to the bedroom shaking her head in desperation.

Bala was aware of the repercussions if he did not make it to where KK was. Suddenly he felt like sinking in a marsh, a feeling of utter helplessness. On one side there was the bully called KK, and on the other side the emotional blackmailing of his dominating wife. Bala had been going through this mental trauma for quite some time now. It was coming to a point where he could not take it anymore.

He stared outside from the balcony of his fourth floor apartment. It was dark like a black-hole, and the air stood still, adding to the misery of high humidity. The mind and the body both he felt were rotting in hell. "What for all this?" the leaves and the red flower petals of the Tulip tree across the balcony seemed to be asking him. He suddenly surged forward succumbing to the urge to jump off from the balcony as invited by the tree. But something was pulling him back. His daughter's fluffy teddy bear had stuck its tail in between the buckles of his capris and was not allowing him through the balcony door. For a moment, the teddy appeared to have his daughter's face, pulling him back to good sense.

Chapter 2

Madame Namy Ferrao came out of the age-old Church with teary eyes. It was their first wedding anniversary since her husband was paralysed in a helicopter crash. She had been an ardent devotee of the Lord since then, a complete volte-face to her atheist and communist college days. The Lord had been instrumental in taking her successfully through the many hurdles she had to face in leading her small ship building yard in her husband's absence.

'Waveproof' had had a small beginning a decade back near the Mazagaon dock in Mumbai, repairing foreign ships that had to sail back soon after the repair. The urgency and desperation of the foreign vessels to leave the shores to meet their commitments was a God-sent opportunity to Waveproof. It minted money, though requiring round-the-clock efforts. In just about five years, it had touched the Rs 500 crore turnover mark that catapulted it onto the burgeoning league of midsized companies eager to be part of the India story.

After touching this magic figure, Jeremy Ferrao felt uncomfortable to be known as a ship-repairer. The tag of a 'ship-repairer' did not give him the required status in the famous Bombay club. He was aware that, behind his back, people called him *'kaatne pootne wala'*, meaning a cutting and welding fellow.

That made him venture out into ship-building, a high capital business. In no time, Waveproof became the darling of ship-liners from this eastern part of the world. What had started off as manufacturing of small oil tankers for the state-owned oil corporation, soon bloomed to become a manufacturer of gigantic container ships for American shipping companies. In the next five years, the company touched a sales turnover of Rs 4500 crores, a growth never seen before in the entire Indian corporate history.

Jeremy was as hard working as before, the novae-riche status or the unprecedented success not going to his head. And it was his personal tradition to deliver the newly built ship to the customer himself. What he normally did was to take his customers, usually accompanied by their near and dear ones, and their key employees for the maiden voyage into the high seas. It was a test ride that also doubled up as one for pleasure. Jeremy also insisted on bearing the costs of the voyage when they sailed towards the seas. His only condition was that the customer bear the expenses of the return trip if and only if they were satisfied with the ship Jeremy's company had built (it was rarely otherwise).

It was during one of those trips into the seas that a Polish customer took objection to the manoeuvrability of the ship. The ship's aft dragged like an unwilling buffalo when subjected to right angle turns at full speed. Jeremy was furious, not at the customer, but at his own technicians.

Since there was a considerable amount of risk in maiden voyages to the seas, a helicopter was always parked on the deck, in case of an emergency. By God's grace, Jeremy had never had to use it though, thanks to the six sigma quality standards maintained ruthlessly in the shop. But this time, it was an emergency. He climbed on to the machine and in no time the bird took its flight towards his Colaba Headquarters that had a beautiful helipad on the terrace.

Helicopter flights to Mumbai take a route adjoining the southern Mumbai coast to avoid the busy airport traffic. And they maintain a very low altitude, as per the DGCA regulations. All these became a blessing in disguise for Jeremy when the helicopter faltered and plunged into the coastal waters barely a kilometre from the shore. Being very near to the naval centre, it was his good fortune that expert rescue teams arrived swiftly to take out the bodies from the floating machine. Jeremy was among the only three people who survived, but the crack on his spine paralysed him for the rest of his life.

Chapter 3

Sixteen hundred years ago, Azerbaijan was a pagan kingdom, ruled by an aborigine king. It was indeed a rule reminiscent of the Utopian Mahabali rule in Kerala, India, which ensured egalitarianism and prosperity. Religion was a practical theory with no inhibitions attached in the form of superstitions. They worshipped the moon, since it was the high tide that brought waters to these parched lands. They worshipped the sun because it dried up the salt water and helped them make salt, which in turn brought the riches to the land. They worshipped the wind for it brought the clouds from the sea bringing in the torrential rains after the gruelling summer. No unseen Gods were worshipped, nobody bothered to sacrifice their happiness to placate the Gods. Religion was just a thanksgiving exercise.

But far down south, religion had taken the shape of a monster. A Roman king, in his selfish pursuit of safeguarding his throne, started forcing a Semitic belief on the unsuspecting citizens. Their age-old practices and beliefs were banished by law. Those who were adamant to hold on to their beloved practices had to leave the land to avoid torture. The king had managed highly systematic campaigners for enforcing Semitism, such that the Pagans had no way but to succumb or to go into exile.

Soon, like a cancer, Semitism spread beyond the Roman Empire, carving on to the heavenly peace that prevailed in Azerbaijan. It all started with the clergymen who came as charity providers. They nurtured the lepers for free, educated the beggars, and trained the scavengers to fish. Slowly but steadily, the clergy made their foot-hold strong, showing their true colours when they gave an ultimatum to the Pagans. 'Fall in line or flee'– the message was clear.

Much to the dismay of the Pagan king, most of the folks succumbed to the pressures of the clergy, thus abandoning their age-old faith as they joined the new order. At the end of the day, the king had only a yacht-full of people who were determined not to bow their heads to the cultural hegemony of the clergymen. And they started crossing the Caspian Sea in a yacht, the wind taking them away from the land they always called their home.

From the frying pan to the fire, they decided when they thought of the hostility that awaited them on the shores of Iran. The barbaric tribes of the desert would pose a physical danger, they assumed. But the gentle-hearted people from Azerbaijan had friends all across the desert. The Azebaijanis treated the traders that came from the deserts seeking business for their wares with kindness. This kindness was reciprocated when these tribesmen in Iran offered them safe refuge and a means of transport to cross the desert. The camels that took them across could have felt the numbness of these minds that had nothing but courage as the only asset with them.

The moon worshippers they were; the tribesmen used to call them 'stargazers'. The stargazers were delighted when these supposedly barbaric tribesmen presented them with well-made wooden boats when they reached the shores of the Arabian Sea, which was then widely known as Sindhu Sagar.

On their queries on the genesis of the name of Sindhu Sagar, it came out that towards east of this sea lay a land that had a history of confluence. A land that had never invaded but had imbibed all incoming cultures and nurtured them. The group that was apprehensive of their acceptance elsewhere thought that there was no better place of refuge than this land.

It was a voyage of their lives; more than the wind, it was the courage and passion for life that had guided their boat towards the coast of India, Goa to be precise. The team of stargazers was mesmerised by the scenic beauty of Goa; the tranquil seas, the serene beaches and the never-ending greenery made them fall in love with this land from the very sight of it from the seas.

Chapter 4

There were a few fishermen who assembled around the Azerbaijanis with their boats and gave a synopsis of the people and the rulers of this land. Prima facie, it was encouraging. But once bitten, twice shy. The captain of the group wanted to take no chance with a foreign territory. Hence, he sent a representative to the ruler of the land–the chieftain of the local tribe.

The messenger was welcomed with suspicion by the land chieftain. Rightfully so, because the land had seen many invasions who but first had come to do business with friendly faces. Is history going to repeat, the question lingered in the chieftain's mind.

With the help of the accompanying fishermen, the chieftain had effectively communicated to the messenger that they could not accommodate foreigners. And as a parting gift, the chieftain gave a coconut to the messenger to be gifted to the captain. It was a customary gift from the people of the region, which symbolised regret and their inability to entertain the visitors' intentions; the coconut represented this message effectively because it is fully sheathed and has no room for outside elements.

What the intelligent captain did was phenomenal. He drew a small hole through the coconut, took out the nectar inside and distributed it to all his people in the presence of the accompanying fishermen. He told the fishermen, "We are a community that will live without disturbing you.

Please give this coconut back to your chieftain and tell him that it is intact even after having served our purpose."

The chieftain was surprised at this and heartily welcomed the group to his land. The group, like all refugees and emigrants who will outperform the locals due to sheer survival instincts, excelled in whatever area they set their eyes on. The locals started revering them and soon counted them as one of those high Brahmin sects whose racial superiority was beyond questions.

Being moon-worshippers, the Azerbaijanis set up a moonorium that was to be the central place of worship for the coming generations. Dark-skinned locals were kept away from the moonorium to ensure the purity of the place. A golden plate, resembling the moon, was embedded on the roof and shined throughout the day and night, depending on the amount of light that fell on it.

The descendants of the dark-skinned local villagers started feeling inferior to these fair-skinned creatures, who also had a better physique than them, and started calling them Chandravanshis, which later became Chandrajas. The Chandrajas focussed on a handful of industries that went with their heritage in mineral excavation, maritime prowess and metal industries.

Later on, when the British ruled India, the white men had a special trust for these fair-skinned Chandrajas, allowing them to prosper with their industries. When the British left India, they'd ruined her self-respect, the riches and the history of this land. The Chandrajas, however, had developed as the numero uno business community of the country.

Chapter 5

Bala came to the office late after having toiled early morning in the school for the various admission-related procedures. Given that the office was always prone to grapevines and rumour mongers, Bala felt uneasy with the looks that awaited him. That was when he actually thought about the late night phone call, the thought that instantly killed the euphoria about his daughter's coveted admission.

There was a note left by the receptionist on the table. "Urgent sales review meeting called at HO tomorrow morning sharp at 8:45." The receptionist, out of her usual flirting habit, had left a Jasmine flower on the note. She had this habit of wearing bunches of Jasmine flowers in her hair and lure men with their romantic fragrance. Bala, a decision maker at the area office, was very much in her radar. She had this uncanny ability to keep these men guessing about her intentions and thus get her work done.

Bala rushed to her seat to get more information about the meeting and who had contacted her. Shiny could very cleverly flash her cleavage in a seemingly innocent way to raise the adrenaline of men, which she did to perfection this time too. Bala managed to stay all business, not giving in to the temptation she was luring him into. KK, he knew, never missed an opportunity to speak to Shiny. And as he had expected, KK had called her up and given the orders for the meeting.

Bala's mind started running like a hare. The only flight that connected Hyderabad to Mumbai was to depart at 11:30 hrs; in those days, flights weren't as frequent as they are today. He looked at his watch, it was already 10:15 and catching that flight was ruled out. If he took an overnight train, he'd be late for the meeting. He had hardly 20 hours to reach Mumbai, since he had to catch a few hours of sleep before freshening up and getting ready for the meeting.

He knew it was tough but couldn't help glancing at his ever-reliable partner. His brick red Hyundai Santro had never let him down. He quickly pulled in his IBM ThinkPad and rushed to his home. Shoving his clothes inside the brand new VIP overnighter and locking the house with the spare key, he was wondering where the hell his wife had gone to. Fortunately, he could overhear the voices from the neighbouring door and recognized his wife's unique husky voice. She had already started talking about the new school syllabus to the nosy neighbour.

He ignored her yelling and shouted back at her, citing her objection to meet KK in the night caused all this mayhem. Without waiting for her to bounce back from that recoil, he sped away quickly.

Chapter 6

Waveproof faced unanticipated testing times ahead. In a span of 18 months, three ships made by them had sunk. This made many customers cancel their orders. There were many conspiracy theories doing the rounds in Mumbai's elite circle. One such theory talked about the role of the CIA; the intention was to bring down a group that would have become a major threat to the American ship makers. Another theory said a rival group in India, belonging to a friend turned foe, must have done this to settle personal scores. Another bizarre theory started talking about mysterious forces, of the Bermuda Triangle type, around the Mumbai coast. This theory for sure was going to gain momentum with the course of things to come.

Waveproof had to make some tough decisions to tide out of this crisis. Namy decided to take up the challenge head on. Some of the choices she had to make were really testing. The immediate course of action was to cut costs. Downsizing manpower was an emotional issue. Like all proprietors, Waveproof also believed in emotionally blackmailing the employees as a retention strategy. Every key employee had direct access to Jeremy to make them feel special and develop a sense of belonging. And this was done without any hierarchical constraints. Even a graduate engineer trainee, if identified to be a promising talent, was cleverly handled by Jeremy. He took a keen interest in the individual development of the employees. Such employees were sent for training at various institutes, sometimes even overseas. Every time, any of these employees put in their papers, Jeremy would cry, as if he was parting with a piece of his heart. Most of the youngsters fell for these crocodile tears.

At the end of the day, Waveproof always boasted of a talent pool without much attrition.

Another strategy was to outsource some of the bulk fabrication jobs. Fabrication jobs needed a large manpower and the overheads of an organised company were always costly. Vendors from the unorganised sector did this job at one-third the cost. This prompted the management to decide in favour of outsourcing. But this meant removing a large chunk of the existing manpower, hitherto held close to heart. A major issue was that Jeremy's emotional mask would come off in the process.

But Namy decided to be the villain and take the blame. She ruthlessly terminated more than a hundred employees, sending shockwaves across the country. The news of Waveproof going for the axe, despite being a benchmark for employee welfare, was taken with sheer surprise by the market and the society.

The outsourcing initiative saved costs for the company by about 30%, which initially boosted the net profit. A sudden boost in the profit was celebrated by the stock market as well as the management with much aplomb.

The euphoria but lasted only for a couple of years.

Soon the news that Waveproof was outsourcing critical fabrication jobs spread like wild fire in the foreign markets. It was spread by the competitors who always carried a dagger at the back. The truth was that Waveproof had never outsourced critical fabrication of important equipment like the hull. It had outsourced only non-pressurized structures such as the internals of the ship. But the news created a lot of hype in the media, and was misinterpreted largely. Soon, the foreign shipping companies started disqualifying Waveproof from their supplier list.

Sudden cancellations and paucity of new orders hit the company like a double whammy. Share prices plummeted. Banks started keeping a distance. The famous Bombay Club refused to renew their membership, this time in Namy's name. Employees who already had seen through the loyalty mask, started leaving in toto. Eventually, even Namy, in her mind, had written off Waveproof.

Chapter 7

Bala's relation with his precious red Santro was something reminiscent of the famous Disney story, and also a motion film, 'Love Bug'. The car had sometimes honked on its own, when Bala had dozed off while still at the wheels. Another day, Bala's daughter Gauri, when she was a toddler, had accidentally opened the door while the car was on the move. But the car all of a sudden, skidded to the opposite side and unknowingly the driver halted the car. The child was saved. Saroja sometimes went overboard with her acquaintances talking about the car's supernatural powers, putting off many of them. "She and her bloody car", they used to murmur behind her back.

But this belief in her car was exactly what gave her solace, when she was thinking about what must have transpired in the office and in what mental state her husband must have been driving all night. She decided to set her worries aside and was relieved and happy to see Gauri running to her, alighting from the school van.

Bala filled the petrol tank, prayed to God and started the car. Starting from Jubilee Hills, Yousouguda, Sanath Nagar, Kukatpally, it took him about an hour to reach the outskirts of Hyderabad from his home because of the traffic.

It was 3 in the afternoon and Bala, having started at 11 in the morning, was feeling hungry. The breakfast of a few *idli* was not enough to compensate the calories he was burning because of the mental turmoil he was going through.

His initial enthusiasm to drive had now died down owing to a burning stomach and the rough roads. Like all rural areas, children in their half knickers started running behind the car as he slowed down seeing a roadside eatery. He was worried that these urchins would tamper with his coveted asset while he was hurriedly going through what was available to eat.

He settled for a bowl of curd rice, some pickle, a green chilli and a glassful of *rasam*. Being closer to the Maharashtra border, he thought that this could be one of the last eateries to serve curd rice, which was a typical south-Indian delicacy. This thought made the curd rice dearer and tastier, or maybe it was the acute hunger that made him gorge on a second helping too. Having no expectation of finding a decent restaurant till he reached Sholapur, he gulped in two cups of black tea before getting behind the wheel again. This, he knew, would stand him in good stead to fight any tendencies of having a siesta.

He thanked those two cups of black tea once he drove into a roadside inn just at the outskirts of Sholapur. This stretch of road was a notorious one because of the number of accidents that took place there regularly. And true to its notoriety, he witnessed a couple of crashes caused by the rough terrain mixed with the drooling eyes of the truck drivers. The poor drivers, who were under tremendous pressure from their owners to deliver the consignments in time, had to drive extra hours under the severe heat of the afternoon sun and the red-hot engine. And these drivers always believed a shot of country liquor would keep them more attentive. The result, however, are the innumerable accidents and deaths that are reported on the Indian roads. Indian roads account for more deaths than all the other accidents, diseases, crimes, and wars in the country put together.

Gulping in the ubiquitous *Masala Dosa* with a pair of *Medu Vada*, he observed the hand carts pulled by the unfortunate ones. They were carrying pilgrims to the nearby temple of Shri Shivyogi Siddeswar. Poor ones helping the fat and unhealthy ones to reach their gods. Who will ferry these poor ones when they soon become ill?

What a fall for a town that was competing with Ahmedabad and Mumbai for the sobriquet of 'Manchester of the East'. What an irony that neither Manchester, Ahmedabad, Mumbai nor Sholapur carried that heritage any more. Surat, considered an underdog, had marched over these rivals. May be Manchester today would want to become the 'Surat of the West'. Sholapur's flagship shawls and the GI tag it carried became a paper tiger due to bad marketing and the general backwardness of the region. Instead, the plethora of sugar mills dominated the horizon with the acute smell of molasses and the mushrooming distilleries. An erstwhile happy population, much reminiscent of the concept of Gandhiji's *Panchayati Raj*, was now being pushed into rampant alcoholism and resultant liver cirrhosis.

Beep! Beep! An SMS from KK's secretary to remind him of the meeting shook him out of his thoughts.

Chapter 8

Ramaswamy had just returned after his long speech at the Singapore Management Association's annual programme for corporate excellence. Ramaswamy was the Chief Operating Officer of Swan Carriers, Singapore's major ship manufacturer. Ram, as he was lovingly called, was a turnaround artist. He took over as the shop head when Swan was getting relegated to the corners by ruthless competitors from Korea and China. The Korean chaebols of Hyundai and Samsung brought quality at such affordable prices that no serious buyer looked at Swan, whose prices were at least 10 % more than the Koreans. Why pay extra for a non-existent quality difference? This question hampered Swan's sales and worried its top bosses.

Ram was a greenhorn as far as the shipping industry was concerned. Hence, when he threw an idea to Swan's management on how he could revolutionize the shipping industry, nobody took it seriously. But Kim Woo Kai, the mercurial CEO of Swan, a person of Japanese origin but settled in Singapore, was known for his impeccable ability to judge people. So, when he saw this young man with brilliant eyes, calling for attention in one of those brainstorming sessions, he had noted down the name.

Ram was surprised that the CEO had called him up to discuss an idea, which had been otherwise out rightly rejected by the old men's gang that was the top management. He had even decided not to waste any more time convincing the old men since they would not be open for new ideas. The sudden call from Kai helped Ram brush aside the negativity and his heart once again started pumping with fresh enthusiasm.

Kai's office had all the doings of aristocracy. Located on the 29th floor of one of the iconic skyscrapers overlooking the harbour, the office gave a panoramic view of the famous Singapore coast line. It had a plush waiting area with beautiful secretaries moving around. The maple wood floor and the sandalwood furniture added to the aristocratic charm. But what took visitors' breath away was the famous Raja Ravi Varma painting—Nair lady adorning her hair—which was clearly visible from the waiting area. Ram was surprised to see this artistic marvel adorning the walls of a Japanese CEO.

"Enthundu Vishesham! (What's up)" Ram was shocked to hear the CEO of Singapore's flagship company greet him in his mother tongue, Malayalam. Reading his mind, Kai explained that he had been an exchange student in Regional Engineering College, Calicut as part of the Insead program. As part of the program, he had spent six months there, during his post-graduation in Rotating Equipment Design from Massachusetts Institute of Technology, USA. That explained his awareness and love for Raja Ravi Varma, Ram realized as he joined the dots, and moved into Kai's office along with him.

"So, tell me about your idea. You Indians are counted next only to the Jews in intelligence. I'm sure your idea will at least be worth a hearing." Kai settled down on his revolving chair after having poured a steaming lemon tea for Ram.

Far away on the sea, as clearly visible through the glass window of the office, a freight ship was puffing out smoke just like the steam coming out from Ram's teacup. Ram smiled gently at the coincidence and turned to face Kai's inquisitive face, the smile remaining on his lips.

"What is the maximum number of years that we expect our ships to ply in the sea?"

The unexpected question from Ram left Kai speechless for a moment. He frowned. Kai was a very sensitive person, and his face was a true reflection of his mind. He tried to understand Ram's intention behind the question, the internal turmoil visible on his face.

"You know it Ram, it is 30-35 years. Why are you asking me?" Kai was still clueless about Ram's thought process.

Ram fished out some papers from his suitcase and highlighted some parts with a green highlighter. He then handed over the two sheets to Kai.

"Would you mind explaining this?" Kai looked at Ram like a schoolteacher waiting for his student to explain his assignment.

Ram had assimilated the data of some fifty shipping companies in the world. The data was analysed to see the average age of ships from the time of inception to the time of breaking. The average age of ships, as per usage, was 21 years. This included the ships that were relegated due to outdated technologies and design defects. Ram's point was that Swan, by designing ships for more than 35 years of operation, was unnecessarily adding up to the costs, making their price unviable in the market.

Customers were ready to pay a decent premium, considering the brand value of Swan. But the price difference of ten percent, compared to its competitors, was not justified, since no customer envisaged their ships to sail for more than 35 years. Ram had collected the data of Swan's competitors too. None of the contract documents asked for a longevity of 35 years. In fact, the contract conditions mentioned shorter durations, ranging from 10-15 years only. The rest of the life ensured for the ships was nothing but goodwill and proof of the product's quality. "Then why design your product for such longevity that no customer is ever going to test?" Ram questioned.

Kai was impressed but did not show it on his face. Typical of a person of Japanese origin, he was very conservative when it came to business decisions. And reticent too, when it came to genuinely praising others. And again, like a typical Japanese, he stood and bowed, a signal for Ram that the meeting was over. Ram also bowed before saying bye. In a sudden turn of events, however, Kai embraced Ram. Going by protocol, it was a gesture out of the way. It showed that Kai was really impressed.

Chapter 9

Bala's red Santro successfully carried him through the risky night driving and by early dawn he was already on the iconic Pune-Mumbai Expressway. He wanted to stop down for a cup of tea, but the expressway did not allow such shops on either side. That forced him to drive on.

He was nearing Lonavla, the beautiful climate and the natural chill making him put off the AC and open the windows. Dew was wetting the windscreen but was drying up his lips making them crack. Bala was starting to feel the fatigue when he saw a Neeta Volvo bus zoom ahead. The tyres of the bus created such a spray from the moist roads, it created a mist adding up to the dew. Bala struggled to see what was ahead of him and hit a side rack because he couldn't see the curve. The car took a sharp right turn due to the impact and was radially crossing the busy expressway from the slower to the faster lane. A dumbstruck Bala could only hear the shrieking tyres of various vehicles but was amazed to see the small car manoeuvring itself amongst the braking vehicles. When he could finally regain some amount of dexterity, the car was already on the slower lane running at a speed of forty kilometres. The only flipside of the whole situation was the earful he had to hear from the other drivers.

Sitting in a scenic Lonavla restaurant, beside the lovely training centre of ICICI bank, Bala was confused whom to give the credit to. The subconscious mind that drives us ahead when its conscious counterpart is down. Or his adorable love bug, which had once again mysteriously added another credit to its credentials. The steaming cup of tea, a fuming cigarette and an early morning breath, all were competing to produce the maximum smoulder around him. Maybe they were all compensating for the smoke that would've otherwise emanated from a pyre.

The car had a huge dent on the front-left with the lights broken completely. He was in a dilemma whether to risk driving the car to Mumbai as it was. Mumbai was a high security area, and he figured that the roads would be subjected to maximum scrutiny. A car with a dent, obviously from an accident, would be subjected to maximum harassment. He wanted to avoid it. But getting the dent removed and the head lights working was going to take time. The sun was yet to rise and there was no way he could find a mechanic so early in the morning. Bala started cursing the God Shanidev, who he thought was responsible whenever he got stuck up like this. He prayed to Lord Hanuman by reciting the *Hanuman Chalisa*. Then he prayed to Lord Ganpati crossing his hands and holding his ears. According to belief, Shanidev is so friendly with Lord Hanuman that he spares whoever prays to his friend. And the same Shanidev is so afraid of Lord Ganpati that he does not dare to touch anyone who prays to Ganpati.

Bala finally decided to park his car in front of a closed garage. He spoke to the garage owner whose cell number was displayed on the shutter gate. He explained his plans and agreed to pick up the car on his way back after two days.

Soon, he had boarded one of those very frequent PuneMumbai shuttle Volvo buses.

Chapter 10

The real challenge for Kai was to convince the board members for the change suggested by Ram. The board members were highly conservative when it came to change in company policy, vehement against any change in the design parameters. They argued that the reputation of the company was at stake if word went out that Swan's ships were no longer designed for a long duration. It required Kai's skills in persuasion to bring them in line. As a trump card, Kai showed the financial projections with the design change and without it. The projections with change showed rich dividends for the stakeholders and it struck a chord with all directors, they being large stakeholders. And needless to say, without design change the company was sinking towards doom and the financial losses had already started affecting the directors' revenues. And who wants to compromise their self-interest for an uncertain tomorrow?!

It was a rigorous schedule for Swan for the next two years. There was a complete design metamorphosis. The confidentiality of the process was maintained to the hilt. Hence, after two years, when the first ship designed as per the new design norms sailed out, the competition never got a whiff of it. They just thought Swan had undergone a price cut to gain orders in the wake of a continuous lull of orders.

But what started as a gentle breeze took the form of a storm very soon. Swan started garnering orders left and right. The world was stunned when the Danish giant, Maersk, placed an order of fifty ships with Swan for a staggering sum of 3.5 billion US dollars. Although this was way below the expected market price, the collaboration was going to do Swan a great deal of good.

Maersk's order turned the tide against the competitors. Like a flock of sheep that follows the shepherd, most of the shipping companies followed the market leader Maersk. Soon, Swan was enjoying a commanding market share of over 55% in the world market. Harvard Business Review hailed this as the biggest comeback story of the decade, with a special focus on Kai's transformational leadership. Kai was spoke of in the same league as Steve Jobs, Larry Page and Jack Welch. The accolades that followed included a hefty bonus from the board and an extension of five more years as the CEO.

However, nowhere did anybody hear the mention of Ram.

Ram was not a man who would take shit from anyone. He waited for some time, hoping that he will be rewarded for his contribution. But in fact, Kai promoted Ram's colleague, the CFO of the company, as one of the directors. That was the proverbial last nail in the coffin for Ram.

Citing the reason of an ailing mother, Ram left Swan and was soon on his way back to India.

Chapter 11

Namy Ferrao was looking up one of her executives who had completed a certificate course in leadership development from the fabled Indian Institute of Management, Ahmedabad. Jeremy had spent fifteen lakhs on him, and hence she wanted to know what he had learned there. The student started blabbering jargons in a typical management graduate's style, which pissed-off Namy. Namy, in her typical gentle demeanour, said that she wanted to see his submission papers to the institute.

She was always critical of Jeremy when it came to his liberal way of spending on his employees' learning and training, without probing much on the potential of candidates and the expected returns. Namy had registered a first impression about the student already; she thought of him as useless. But just as a formality, she was glancing through his submissions. There, she chanced upon a case study on Swan Ship Builders, the world's largest ship manufacturing company. She pulled it and began to read it.

The case study spoke about how Swan, a year back, was turned around by a genius called Ram, who happened to be an alumnus of IIM, Ahmedabad. Prof. Parikh, who had written the case study, on which the student had to do an analysis of various scenarios, had a reference to the CEO, Mr Kai also. Among the many things that needed to be analysed, an important question was, who really deserved the credit. The CEO or the COO. Namy suddenly thought about the political debate she had seen on a news channel on whether it was erstwhile prime minister, Narasimha Rao, or his finance minister, Manmohan Singh, who deserved to be called the architect of the Indian Economic reforms. In the early nineties, India was on the brink of an economic meltdown and the government was planning to mortgage the gold reserves to tide over a fiscal crisis. The International Monetary Fund and other financing agencies agreed to bail out the economy from this grave crisis, but on a condition. The condition was that India should liberalize the economy and open up for foreign investments. The hitherto regime of high import duties had to go and reforms of free economy had to be brought in. Rao knew that, if this game is not played really well, the country would be an economic slave to international agencies. And only a financial whiz kid can make this happen for the country. His choices were all politicians as finance ministers. He took a huge political risk by side-lining all political heavyweights for the coveted post and made an academic expert, Manmohan Singh as the finance minister. The rest is history as they say, as India became an economic power house thereafter.

A fleeting thought may be, but she saw a similarity between the two cases. Namy went through the case study as if she was the student. Then she discussed with the young man about his interpretation of the case, what others in his class had opined, and, finally, what was the Professor's take on the case. Indicating a total change in her mood, she ordered for two cups of cappuccino. Sipping on the coffee, but not muttering a word, she went through the case many more times. And then, as if she had finally come to a decision, she let the student leave her office.

It didn't take much time for Namy to connect to the Director of IIMA. Having sent a couple of students for courses there every year, the Director was always happy to speak to her. Namy directly came to the point. She wanted to know the whereabouts of Ram. The director at once called for the professor in charge of the alumni cell, Professor Nikhil Parikh. The professor was also the author of that case study. When it came to the details of his star alumni, Nikhil had them on the tip of his tongue. Moreover, the success story of Swan was a hot topic in the business circles.

There was a story in the Indian epic, *Mahabharat*. Arjun, the great warrior, along with his four brothers and their wife Panchaali was subjected to 14 years of exile. Out of the 14 years, the last year had to be in disguise. The exile was a result of a game of dice that they lost while gambling with their cousin and bête noire Duryodhan.

During this time, if anybody found out of their whereabouts, they would have to go into another 14 years of exile.

Their enemies, the Kauravas, therefore, kept a strict watch to find out about their cousins.

During this clandestine year, they took refuge at the palace of a local king on the peripherals of the jungle. Having known of their presence through spies, the Kauravas decided to attack this king.

The king's son, an amateur prince with youthful energy, took up the challenge and decided to take on the enemy to protect his father, the king. The prince, who was being taught archery by Arjun (disguised as a eunuch), insisted that Arjun be his charioteer. The king and his courtiers scolded the prince and ridiculed him for taking a eunuch for the battle.

But the prince's obstinacy prevailed and both of them, along with a small army, started for the battleground. But after coming face to face with the formidable force of the enemy, which included the world's best warrior Karna among others, the adolescent prince lost all his steam. He wanted to run away from the battle ground.

Arjun tried his very best to keep the morale of the prince high but to no avail. The prince was hell bent on doing an about-turn. Arjun looked at the sky and with an inherent smile on his face led the chariot towards the large banyan tree under which he had hidden his arms. The moon had set on the western horizon and it marked the end of the 14 years of exile, as per the lunar calendar. The prince's mouth dropped when he saw Arjun's priceless bow, the *Gaandiva*. Arjun tightened the string of the bow and did a mock test. The swirls of the air created such a huge thunderous sound that the enemy instantaneously guessed who it was. Arjun asked the prince to be his charioteer and raced to the battleground where the enemy was making a free advance. *Gaandiva* was vibrating at its brilliant best and the enemy had no option but to run away. Arjun's repeated mock test of the *Gaandiva* with its thunderous roars reiterated his identity. It reminded the retreating enemy that the 14 years were over and he was now scot free.

Back to the palace, the news of the prince having won spread like a wild fire. But the king knew fully well who must have won the war. Because by that time, the king's secretary (who happened to be Arjun's eldest brother, Yudishtir) had spilled the beans of who the eunuch really was.

Professor Nikhil Parikh was feeling somewhat like this king. Having known Ram from his college days, Nikhil had no doubt about who must have turned around Swan. Kai's success story was only reminiscent of that poor prince. After all, Ram was from IIM Ahmedabad (IIMA), India's answer to Harvard and Stanford.

Chapter 12

Bala's bus puffed and panned its way through the heavy Mumbai morning traffic to reach Chembur. It was already 8.30 and he had to reach the office and get freshened up in 15 minutes time. He rushed to get an auto and shouted "Waveproof towers" to the waiting auto drivers. Nobody showed interest since it was just half a kilometre from there. "You want me to take an auto to Dubai from here?" he muttered cursing them and moved forward to show hands to a passing biker.

Mumbai stands out among Indian cities in terms of discipline and helping out each other. The best example can be seen from the orderly queues to board the BEST buses. A camaraderie can be seen in the local trains where people hold the ones clinging on from the doors from being hit by passing electrical posts. Also, Mumbaikers were lion-hearted when it came to helping fellow citizens during the Mumbai floods. One of the bikers was gracious enough to help the middleaged man desperately asking for a lift.

Rushing into the seventh floor rest-room for freshening up, Bala was ready in his formals after a quick shave and a wash in flat five minutes. Spraying his deodorant on his way to the reception, Bala obliviously emptied the whole can of Axe Signature deodorant. Going by the popular ad that showcased the deodorant as the one used by '*chick magnets*', the receptionist squinted with surprise at Bala. Bala understandably was in no condition to think of romance and the loaded looks from the lady did not register with him at all.

Having struggled to reach Mumbai, Bala had not thought about the very purpose he had travelled all the way. But now, resting on the plush sofa with his back against the AC duct, reality started sinking in. How was he going to counter KK? He pulled out his laptop and while it was booting, he asked the receptionist by when KK was expected to be free. KK was yet to arrive in office, the receptionist told him. "Oh, another late night drinking session," he thought with contempt on his face.

Bala, in the meantime, made notes in his diary. But due to lack of sleep the previous night and the fatigue of driving throughout, and also because of the chilled air from the AC duct, he fell asleep with the laptop still on his lap. He was in deep slumber when he was abruptly shaken awake by the receptionist, who was now looking tensed. He could hear expletives, distinctly from Hyderabad, being showered on him from a distance, from somebody who was moving away from him. It took a few seconds for him to come to his senses. "KK is pissed off at you and wants me to kick you out from here," the receptionist told with remorse. It was, perhaps, the effect of his deodorant that had prevented her from doing so.

"Hi Bala, what are you doing here?" A friendly voice suddenly brought him out from his thoughts. Shikhar Khetrapal was standing with the airs of yesteryear movie star, Dev Anand, his head slightly tilted. Shikhar was the Head of Service for Waveproof. Bala was working under him in Mumbai before he got transferred to Sales. Bala was reluctant to move to Sales or to shift from Mumbai, but for his wife Saroja's persistence. Nowadays, whenever he got into trouble with KK, Bala blamed his wife for her stubbornness that had landed him in this mess. Bala always reminded her of the good days he had working under Shikhar, touring the world at the company's expense.

Bala explained Shikhar what brought him to Mumbai, highlighting the torturing travel. Shikhar and KK had a long rivalry behind them. Having brought up from the same cadres, they grew together like a pair of twins. If Shikhar was known for his flamboyance, KK was famous for his clinical approach. Never talk anything without back data, was KK's mantra. Shikhar, on the other hand, was outspoken and quite often bluffed to keep pace with KK. But the gift of the gab and a little amount of bullying always saved the day for him. If Shikhar was in awe of KK's methodical approach, KK had an inferiority complex towards Shikhar's exuberance and good looks. As they grew up in the organisation, so did the sycophants around them. This added to their rivalry in bringing more prominence to their protégés. Needless to say, Bala was Shikhar's blue-eyed boy. So, when KK played a dirty game to snatch Bala away from Shikhar, Shikhar was planning since to strike back.

Once Bala had explained his ordeals of working under KK, Shikhar battled with an urge to take revenge. Two consecutive cigarettes could not cool him down. He rushed into his cabin, Bala following him. Shikhar picked up his Rubik cube, which he was very fond of, and fiddled with it. Bala was waiting for a response, his tension visible on his face.

The ringing of the phone called for their attention. "That swine is calling you. Now go and eat shit," Shikhar told once he kept down the call that was from the reception. "Let me see what I can do," he said, giving Bala some amount of solace before he left for KK's office.

Chapter 13

Ram had landed on Bengaluru's swanky new airport. The weather in Bengaluru was living up to its reputation of being an air-conditioned city. It was the wee hours of a cold morning and the IT capital of India was crawled under the heavy blanket of fog. A fog created more of vehicle pollution than the dew. The Singapore Airlines flight had just emptied down its load and the engines were enjoying a respite before it took off again to Singapore. Passengers were lazily inching towards the exit area like the ghosts of the popular Michael Jackson album, Thriller. Looking at the various customs formalities and the disembarkment form to be filled, many a passenger was regretting having come to India. They were those typical NRIs who scowled at anything Indian, the moment they manage to get off the shores of this great country. Ram, however, was very happy to have come back to his homeland. Reminiscent of Swami Vivekananda, he was also thirsting to roll on the soil of his homeland.

Once the formalities were over, Ram got into the famous Vaango outlet to savour the fabled south Indian filter coffee. Extra big *Medu Vada* resembling small muskmelons looked alluring with the hot *Sambhar* boiling in the kitchen, its aroma spreading around. Ram decided to break his fast then and there, ordering one more coffee. The Hindu newspaper, regarded an intelligent man's favourite, gave him good company. The business section of the newspaper carried an article on the catharsis at an Indian ship manufacturing company, Waveproof. A left leaning paper, it focussed more on how the once safe employer was laying off people. It even gave a judgement on Indian managers who did not seem to be good at managing crisis.

Having seen the world, Ram was convinced that Indian managers with their strong ethical background and entrepreneurial thinking were the best managers in the world. The faces of Indra Nooyi, Satya Nadella and Sundar Pichai popped up in his mind. He felt pity for today's journalism that always took leanings.

More than journalism, what pricked his mind even more was the state of the company called Waveproof. Being from the same industry and a person who loved anything Indian, Ram was really unhappy to see the downfall of this small but beautiful Indian company. He was very much in awe of Jeremy Ferrao and remembered having presented a case study on upcoming Indian companies while in IIMA. He had highlighted Waveproof as a company that had the potential to develop as the next Indian multinational. A narcissist, Ram hated when his predictions went wrong.

Gigantic *Medu Vada* and a couple of hot cups of coffee early in the morning propelled him to the loo. Relaxing on the toilet seat, he suddenly thought of the cab driver Sundarappa who must be waiting for him. It had slipped from his mind that he had called up Sundarappa from Singapore to pick him from Bengaluru airport. Sundarappa being his trusted driver never failed to be present whenever Ram had asked him to. Ram was wondering why Sundarappa had not called him when he remembered that he was yet to switch on his iPhone.

He was just browsing through the phone expecting Sundarappa to call any time, when he noticed a message from his old contact in IIMA, Nikhil. He had messaged pleasantries with a request to call him. Maybe it had something to do with setting up guest lectures, he thought.

Sundarappa called just then and soon Ram got into the taxi, falling fast asleep on his way.

Chapter 14

"What the fuck are you up to these days?" KK was at his arrogant best. Bala was mentally prepared for any kind of assault. Knowing KK very well, he was expecting expletives. But KK was very smart. He knew Shikhar must have fed something to Bala. In the age of cell phones and spy cameras, KK was not ready to take a risk in his race with Shikhar for the corner office. KK knew how to play his best within the constraints.

"Come Bala, let us go visit a customer," KK said, gesticulating him to sit down. KK, like all bullies, was an expert in changing colours akin to a chameleon. He suddenly became very courteous, asking Bala if he needed some tea or coffee. Bala could smell trouble in going out with KK. But there was no way he could avoid that. Soon they were on their way out of the office, but not before Bala could sneak out to the loo and send a quick message to Shikhar.

As expected, KK drove towards an infamous dance bar in Wadala. Bala had heard enough of his rendezvous with bar girls. KK had yet another nickname, the snake charmer, because of his heroics in the bar. KK enjoyed girls doing lap dances on him and would throw away thick stashes of notes at them. Hence, there was always a competition for the girls to do the grind on his lap. But KK always loved a particular girl, the one who did a 'Naagin' dance

Bala always felt that dance bars were sheer exploiters of poor women. He was of the type who would not even look at a naked girl, so as not to offend his morals. Like a typical sadist, KK could sense the uneasiness in Bala's mind and was thrilled.

Soon, a sunglasses clad motorcyclist entered the bar without any fanfare and took a seat in a dark corner. It was usual for shy people to take the corners to avoid public attention fearing social stigma. The tall and lanky man had a very strong physique. If not for his white Nike t-shirt, Levi's blue denims, a funky baseball cap and of course the brown wayfarer glasses, anyone could have taken him as a cop or a military man. The demeanour notwithstanding, the waitresses were reticent to approach him. They were, probably, wary of him, a complete stranger. Finally, a girl took up the challenge and approached him. He ordered for a Carlsberg Elephant beer with a plate of cheese-pineapple to gulp it down with. His no-nonsense attitude and the mystic aura kept the girls away from using their usual tricks on him. Pretending to look at something on his iPhone, he was keeping a watch on what was going around.

Meanwhile Bala was waiting for KK to finish his first few pegs. After his 5th peg KK usually got moonstruck. But Bala was disappointed when after KK's third one, he asked Bala to order for food. Sensing Bala's confusion, KK himself called for the waitress and ordered one *'Mutton Biriyani'* for himself and a curd rice for Bala. Bala's love for curd rice was well-known across Waveproof. The handsome hunk from the corner had just crossed over KK's seat on his way to the restroom, pasting his chewing gum on the back of the chair.

Bala was the key account holder for the Indian Navy's ships' refurbishment projects in Vishakhapatnam. Waveproof was one of preferred parties by the Defence ministry to work on these highly sensitive projects. The job involved renovation and modernisation of aged ships. Waveproof was given the most sensitive job of modernisation of the Russian-made submarines. These units were a state secret, since the number of these nuclear submarines was a guessing game for the outside world. For this activity Bala was directly reporting to Ashok Grewal, the CEO.

KK slowly started probing about the prohibited details. He wanted to know the basics of a nuclear submarine, inquisitive as a school boy. Bala, even though aware that he was not supposed to spill the beans, explained the basics of a nuclear submarine, surely knowing KK must be having much deeper knowledge about it.

Before he knew it though, KK started enquiring about other things, like the key personnel working on the project. Bala was wondering whether KK was just nosy or if he had hidden intentions. As if he had read Bala's perplexed mind, KK ended the discussion and asked for the bill.

Chapter 15

Ram's sojourn in Bengaluru was short-lived. His picturesque bungalow in Cambridge Layout overlooking the Sai Temple was so alluring that it always left Ram wanting for more. The recent developments in the area had in fact added to its charm with a classy Café Coffee Day joint and a Crossword book store nearby. Given the nature-lover Ram was, this neighbourhood, with the magnificent Bengaluru weather, always made him wonder whether the 'God's own country' sobriquet really belonged to his home state Kerala or this air-conditioned city of Bengaluru.

Ram was settling in after arriving from Singapore in the early hours of the morning. Saravanan, his care taker, had welcomed him with his signature cup of filter coffee. Ram would publicly praise this filter coffee in whichever part of the world he went to. His bedroom was spick and span, and it was hypnotizing him towards that much needed sleep after the odd timed air travel. Before he fell asleep, however, he thought of going through the pack of mails that had come in his absence. A letter caught his attention.

The letter looked like it was hand written by the revered chair-person of Waveproof Ms Namy Ferrao herself. He picked it up leaving everything aside and went through it. It was a personal invitation to meet her while in India. Ram did not have any particular fascination for Namy since he thought she was more of a show-off and lacked real substance. But being in the same fraternity and also because of Indian penchant, Ram was forced to think over it.

It was evening when he woke up, oblivious of the heavy rains outside. The only other city which was reminiscent of the unpredictable weather in Bengaluru was London. Care taker had brought in a bottle of Bacardi White Rum, a pack of Wills Navy Cut cigarette and some Bharuch peanuts. He didn't forget to bring in the day's The Hindu Newspaper, the intellectual scribes whom Ram loved to read.

Munching on the takeaway *Biryani* from the Hyderabadi Biryani outlet from Queens Road, and sipping on the ultimate combination, Bacardi rum with Thumbs Up, Ram lighted his favourite cigarette from his college days. It reminded him of the grind he had undergone during his 12th standard, his quest for IIT-JEE. Those days only the privileged from the cities could crack the JEE. The 2-year elite course from Brilliant Tutorials was the only solace for rural kids. That large office writing pad was the only witness to his gruelling schedule, which he treasured even now. Other than the occasional heavenly puffs from Wills Navy Cut, the pack that costed only Rs 5 those days, there was no entertainment for him. Except for those masturbations that eased the tension from his mind. He revelled the poster of Samantha Fox that adored the walls of his study room; there was no limit to his fascination for her.

Every time Ram got stuck when making a crucial decision in life, he would regenerate this atmosphere. The Wills Navy Cut and a well imagined hand work injected within him the required chemicals to take a winning decision. And he took one.

Chapter 16

KK continued probing Bala even after the waitress left the bill with them. Bala, like a cat thrown in water, kept on huffing and puffing, somehow giving many hints about the secret project. He was expecting Shikhar to do something but was increasingly getting exasperated with Shikhar's inaction. But soon the executive assistant of the CEO entered the bar. He was tipped off by Shikhar who traced KK and Bala through one of the Graduate Engineer Trainees (GETs) working under him, who was surreptitiously following them on a motorbike.

There was obvious relief on Bala's face when he saw Jigar dropping in at their table saying hello. KK was surprisingly nonchalant. Jigar made some excuse about dropping in at the dance bar. But finally, he had to admit that he had been sent by the CEO on Shikhar's complaint. KK looked at both of them with his ember red eycs and briskly walked out throwing a bundle of notes at the waitress.

But to the utter surprise of both Jigar and Bala, KK was waiting for them outside with a plateful of *'Shingoda sweet paans'*. He allowed Jigar to go back in the company vehicle and gesticulated Bala to join him in his car. Bala was doubting and threw Jigar a confused look. KK, as if reading his mind, solaced Bala. "Don't worry Bala, I never had the intention to hurt you. Please trust me." Bala had to go by those words of consolation and soon they were driving back to office.

That's when KK enquired about how he reached Mumbai and was aghast when Bala told about the gruesome drive and the accident at the end. KK halted the car on the side road out of sheer surprise. "Bala, why on earth did you take such a huge risk, my boy?" KK sounded like a different man altogether. Being part of top management and therefore not having a daily reporting structure, KK chose at once to drive to Lonavla to fetch Bala's car from the garage. On their return to Mumbai, KK handed over an air ticket to Bala to go back to Hyderabad and told his driver to drop the car back to Hyderabad.

The sudden change in KK's demeanour did confuse Bala, but KK was a master in interpersonal skills. He played a master stroke about enquiring the schooling facility available in Hyderabad. The moment he heard that Bala was trying to secure his daughter's admission at the Cathedral school he scolded Bala about not telling him about this beforehand. He called up his close friend Fernando Coutinho, who was a big trader in Hyderabad. Within half an hour there was a call from the school confirming Bala's daughter's admission. Bala was swept off his feet.

He would have done anything to get that admission for his studious daughter. Bala, like any executive who could not make it big and was already in their mid-thirties, was pinning his hopes on the next generation. The software wave had belittled the achievements of the guys in the brick-and-mortar industries. In their mid-thirties, while his software colleagues after having globe trotted were planning to retire and do organic farming or pursue their dreams, Bala and his brick-and-mortar ilk were still worried to buy that flat or save money for the child's education. Software must have been the sunrise sector for the country or at least for a bunch of smart head-starters, but it had loomed large as a depression on the people who missed the bus.

In a couple of days, life was normal for Bala as he finished off the admission formalities, enjoyed a truce with KK and had a content wife at home.

Chapter 17

Namy Ferrao was at her best when it came to aristocratic dressing. The weather was surprisingly pleasant in Goa. The Leela hotel's sea facing suite had to be booked well in advance under normal circumstances. But the continuing sanctions against Russia by the USA on the backdrop of its adventure in Ukraine had broken the economy of many ordinary Russians. To add to that, the new government in Goa was hard hitting at the drug mafia. With drugs getting costlier and the purse shrinking, the Russian flow to Goa dwindled. The hotel rooms were now available at a throwaway price. That was one of the reasons Namy chose Goa, apart from her love for the serenity of the sea and also to avoid the peeping toms in the Mumbai office. She was supposedly on a short holiday.

Ram had checked in to the Ginger Hotel in Panjim, being a worshipper of the great Tatas and also a person who believed in austerity. He quickly went through the buffet breakfast. The food tasted better when a beautiful and courteous hostess moved around among the guests enquiring about their stay. The hotel had arranged a car and soon he was on his way to The Leela.

The balcony protruding from the drawing room of Namy's suite towards Leela's private beach was Ram's choice for the rendezvous, instead of the air-conditioned plush interior. The beach was sporadically filled, given that it was early morning, reflecting the lack of foreign tourists. Ram had brought a gift for Namy. The fabled *Aranmula Kannadi* that was an ancient glassless mirror, a wonder for everyone. One of the many things other than the spices that had attracted the Europeans to this part of the world.

Ram was the one who started talking in his usual exuberant style, wanting to know more about Waveproof. He wanted to understand the grasp Namy had of the precarious situation her company was in. Actually, being a highly methodical man, Ram had collected information and studied about Waveproof already.

The sea was getting warmer, as was the discussion. Namy had ordered for some Black Forest pastries along with some lemon tea. Savouring the lemon tea, Ram thought of the fallacy of high life. The lemon tea, which used to be called *Sulaimani* in his hometown near Palakkad, was a road side item that had a heavenly taste. Coming back to the subject, leaving his wistful thoughts behind, he continued probing Namy about why Waveproof was looking for a new leadership, even though the answer was obvious. But he wanted to gauge the relationship she shared with her top management.

Namy was very sophisticated when it came to interviewing the top brass. She looked at the human elements more than the professional prowess. She struck an instant chord with Ram, who was too simplistic for a CEO. She even hinted at that. She quoted the example of Bill Gates and Ratan Tata, who were famous for their simplicity but carried themselves too well in the corporate and government circles. Simplicity, as a virtue, adorned the rich and famous, but was it possible for the CEO of a mediocre company like Waveproof to be simplistic and still earn respect? Ram did not answer that directly but took the example of Mahatma Gandhi who led an impoverished nation, truly representing it by being half-clad and still commanded the respect of all humanity.

From the discussion, Ram clearly concluded that Waveproof was in dire needs of a world class manager to tide out from its crisis. And Ram also needed a job.

Chapter 18

Bala was soon a part of KK's coterie. They frequently went out together in Hyderabad. Bala, who was a teetotaller earlier, graduated towards beer and wine after persuasion from the bad boys in the group. Saroja, who had never seen Bala coming home after ten in the night, was witness to him coming late very often, that too drunk. Her complaints and advices went in vain and at times Bala abused and threatened her if she irritated him. For the child, he became a Sunday uncle, since she left for school early in the morning and by the time Bala was home at night, she was already asleep. What was once a happy family turned into a fuming pressure cooker, ready to burst any time.

Saroja boasted of a royal pedigree. Her forefathers were the rulers of a southern kingdom before Tipu Sultan made mincemeat of the place. Though the invasion deprived them of their riches, their majestic looks remained. Saroja, who resembled the famous actress Nargis, was a delight to watch. It was Bala's sheer luck and Saroja's compassion for the hard working but poor classmate that drove them towards each other. Whoever saw this couple used to wonder and find solace in the saying, '"Love is blind'. Over the years, Bala had developed an inferiority complex due to people's apparent questioning of their match.

Saroja was used to this kind of slandering and had grown immune to all that. Given her high thinking and the lionhearted person that she was, all the slandering was brushed aside as childish jealousy. Love, after all, overrides every other emotion in the world.

But Bala's attraction to her, like any other male, was waning as the years passed by. Once their child was born, Saroja was no more the same tigress she used to be in bed earlier. Priorities changed and sex was done only to satisfy her husband's urge. The lady, like most other mothers, was more concerned about her precious child's well-being and future. Love had shifted from the mate to the offspring.

Unlike Saroja, Bala always had a frustration that he was nursing inside, though it was well camouflaged by his salesman-like smile and smartness. The calumny had, in fact, made a deep impact in his mind that grew as a foetus of frustration.

Chapter 19

Soon, Waveproof had handed over the submarines to the Navy with a lot of fanfare. It opened the doors for more orders for refurbishment; this time a couple of war ships came in along with a bunch of nuclear submarines. The Government of India's new push for indigenization of defence manufacturing gave an impetus for learning new technologies as a forerunner to replace the foreign companies in the manufacturing of critical ships.

The handing over ceremony was attended by many, including the President of Russia, along with the mercurial Indian Prime Minister who everyone called the lioness. There were already rumours floating around about these two leaders.

The macho and handsome Russian president was famous for his maverick ways, flamboyant life style and his fetish for high profile women. His rendezvous with the Chinese First Lady gave fodder to the paparazzi for many months. Everyone was speculating about this affair. Nobody ever discussed the multi-billion dollar crude oil agreement signed between the Communist country and the Russians. This helped Russians tide over the severe liquidity crisis that had gripped them after the Americans had imposed sanctions on them after their invasion of Crimea in Ukraine. This also helped the Chinese to get a long- term commitment on their crude requirement that would minimize their dependence on sea-borne supplies, which could be under embargo in case of the escalating tensions in the South China Sea.

The lack of media attention helped to push under the carpet the concerns this deal had created in the minds in Washington. To add to the Americans' woes with respect to containing Russia, here it was the turn of an Indian Prime Minister to show bonhomie to the Russian Casanova. The legendary Boney M number kept on playing in the corridors of the Central Intelligence Agency's headquarters.

The lyrics of the Ra Rasputin song echoed in the American minds like that of the Czar Nicholas II. The lyrics went like this:

"There lived a certain man in Russia long ago
He was big and strong in his eyes a flaming glow
Most people looked at him with terror and with fear
But to Moscow chicks he was such a lovely
dear He could preach the bible like a preacher,
full of ecstasy and fire
But he also was the kind of teacher women would desire

Ra-Ra-Rasputin
Lover of the Russian queen
There was a cat that really was gone
Ra-Ra-Rasputin
Russia's greatest love machine
It was a shame how he carried
on
....

....

Ra-Ra-Rasputin
Russia's greatest love machinc
And so they shot him till he was dead.

Oh, those Russians! "

The last line kept giving the Americans sleepless nights for a while.

Chapter 20

Ram soon replaced Waveproof's aging CEO, Ashok Grewal, with the grooming period being a namesake three months. In reality, Ram hit the ground running. After all, do the tiger cubs need to be trained in hunting? Namy knew that more than anyone else, and handed over the reins to who was, arguably, the most talented man in the industry.

She was feeling like what Duryodhan must have felt on the 11th day of the great *Mahabharat* war, when his warrior friend took over the leadership of the Kauravas. Duryodhan was not happy when Bhishma first and Drona controlled the army. He had to go by this protocol of respecting elders. But when the world's best warrior Karna was at the helm of affairs, after the death of Bhishma and Drona, Duryodhan brimmed with confidence for the first time.

And that was exactly how Namy felt. She, after having taken over as the chairperson of Waveproof, never felt that it had an effective CEO whom she could trust with the operations. She was always looking for that person who had Jeremy's poise and acumen.

And Ram, in the first few moments of his joining the office, had won her confidence. The proof of Namy's euphoria came in the form of a brand new, perfect black, Jaguar XL Petrol, which she gifted to Ram. The white-uniformed chauffeur made a good contrast with the shining darkness of the car, his long and black moustache adding to the charm.

But Ram being Ram, the first thing he did was to reject this car and go and buy a ready stock silver Mahindra XUV 500. A man who never allowed his servant to clean his plates, could never fathom the idea of a chauffeur. And driving was the only passion that remained with him after all the corporate years took the sheen out of this yesteryear sprinter. An aspiring Carl Lewis or Usain Bolt was lost to India in its unending quest for doctors and engineers.

Ram's initial assessment of Waveproof was typical and predictable of anyone who has had foreign exposure. Contrary to the management principle called PDCA (Plan Do Check Act), Indians generally and Waveproof particularly had this concept of Do Check Plan Act (DCPA), the reverse. The company did not have a central planning department. Jobs were carried out as and when the machines were free. Vendors were never given a challenging delivery period. The leniency resulted in the vendors taking away non-negotiated prices, that too with a hefty advance amount. This was against the very stringent government payment terms for ship orders that gave no advance; in the rare cases when it was given, it was maximum 10% and that too against a bank guarantee. The fact was that the vendors were all small companies who could not execute an order without advance. But the number of vendors being huge in totality, it put a huge working capital pressure on Waveproof.

When Ram sat with the cash flow analysis after identifying this fundamental problem, the fallout was startling. It was natural for shipping companies to put stringent delivery terms on ship builders. Hence, to be competitive in the market as far as delivery terms were concerned and to keep up its reputation of a company that meets its delivery commitments, Waveproof decided to hold some inventory. All the standard components of a ship were ordered for manufacturing based on projected orders without actually having the orders in hand. Such orders emptied the coffers because of the hefty advances paid to the vendors. By the time a customer paid for the ships, it was more than two to three years depending on the payment terms agreed.

Waveproof was not such a behemoth or a conglomerate that could afford such cash flows. Ram decided to clean the slate and focus on how to revamp vendor management to safeguard cash flows. But it was easier said than done.

It was then that this high IQ man decided to go for a paradigm shift as far as company products were concerned. Hitherto, the company was retrofitting the aging troop of submarines in collaboration with Russians as a top secret Indian defence project. With the core strength of Waveproof in manufacturing ships, Ram was confident of one thing—Waveproof was a clear favourite, if at all an Indian company ventured into submarine manufacturing. Having a running technical collaboration with the Russians and also being in the good books of the Government of India for having kept the confidentiality upright, Ram had no doubts when he mooted this idea of manufacturing submarines to Namy.

As expected by Ram, Namy showed no resistance and was, in fact, overwhelmed by the idea that would open up an additional revenue stream for her company, thereby reducing the dependence on the dog-eat-dog and thankless merchant shipping industry. She nursed a quiet hatred for ships since the mishap of her husband.

Ram had killed two birds with one shot. The additional revenue and the new image of the company was a complimentary benefit. The real benefit was the opportunity to develop a new stream of vendors, who had to be qualified with the highly stringent defence norms. And foreseeing huge business from defence, every vendor wanted to carry that tag of a defence supplier. This enabled Waveproof to have an upper hand during negotiations with them. The vendors not only agreed for a zero advance deal, but also for a credit period of sixty days, hitherto unheard in the industry. It was only a matter of time before the same terms were replicated in the main stream shipping deals as well.

Getting the government's nod was easy, and soon the Technology License Agreement (TLA) was signed during the PM's visit to Moscow with much fanfare. The government was using the deal to trumpet its new initiative of 'Make in India', thereby bringing in foreign capital, technology and jobs to India. As the flagship deal of this initiative, an order for fifty submarines to be supplied over a period of twelve years was promulgated and signed during the visit.

Chapter 21

The TLA signed by the Russians with Waveproof, on behalf of the Indian government, for the making of submarines came as a boon for KK. It gave him the opportunity to travel to St. Petersburg quite a few times. It was a December when KK had to rush to the Russian city to clear off a stalemate with respect to the technology transfer.

A Russian company, Rosmarine, was a veteran in the manufacturing of submarines. It was formed by the erstwhile Soviet Union during the Second World War to tackle the formidable U-boats of the German Navy. Its design, though, was copied from a model stolen from Germany through spies. Though the Americans and the British developed better models and technology rather than harping on a stolen German model, the Russians lagged behind on innovations. Hence, even today, Rosmarine's submarine design was more or less similar to what the Germans designed seventy years back.

The Indian software prowess cutting across all segments was lauded by the world. This was an area where the Indian companies including Waveproof could steal a march over their global rivals and counterparts. So, when it came to submarines being made in India, there were many parts the Indians wanted to be automated with the current software and artificial intelligence technologies. To make it possible the Russians needed to divulge some of their design parameters. This was a stalemate, wherein it was the clash of two generations. One generation that was yet to come out of the laidback iron curtain days of the Soviet Union. The other generation was a computer savvy young Indian generation that had produced world-beaters like Sabeer Bhatia, among many other cyber geeks.

But unlike the stalwarts India had created, KK lacked the moral integrity all of them had displayed. Hence each of his Russian visits was drenched in an overdose of booze. The December visit was also no different.

As expected, December welcomed KK to Russia with an abundance of ice and snow. The cold was piercing his bones, and at times he felt even the best of Vodka would not spare him from this torture. Cold winds had exhausted all his energy by the time he came out of the airport, took a taxi and landed at the hotel lobby.

The hotel lobby looked like a war-museum. It had the remains of a Luftwaffe aircraft that was brought down by the red army during its famous assault on the Nazis. The walls were adorned with various machine guns and heritage weapons. The reception itself was shaped like a tank, its long barrel protruding to the top dome of the lobby, from which hung a chandelier.

The hotel room, specially booked for him by Rosmarine, was warm, as it was centrally heated. It was nearing 1.00 pm, although it looked as if the sun was going to set in few moments. KK had digested whatever breakfast he had consumed in the aircraft and was feeling hungry.

After a quick wash, KK was in a dilemma whether to go for room service or go down to the coffee shop. Before he could decide, the doorbell rang. A lady in a formal dress introduced herself as Tatiana Onoprienko. She said she was from Rosmarine and was sent to make him comfortable. She was concerned about his well-being and expectedly asked about the lunch.

Taty, as she liked to be called, led KK like the proverbial pied piper to the coffee shop. The coffee shop had an elevated bar, with the best of Vodkas on display. The bartenders were, needless to say, gorgeous Russian beauties. And the radiance of these bombshells outglared the magnificent interiors of the bar, which was reminiscent of Nicholas-II, the Czar's, pompous court. KK was, in fact, perplexed whether to look at the drop dead gorgeous Taty or the scantily clad waitresses.

As if to break the ice and as per the general notion about Indians, Taty picked vegetarian items from the menu and pointed them to KK. KK, typically a carnivore, looked at Taty with dismay and grabbed the menu from her. But nothing in the menu resembled a *Chicken Tikka* or a *Hyderabadi Biriyani.* It talked of some fancy names that Taty later clarified as pig or bear meat. KK resigned to the fact that he had to be satisfied with vegetarian food when he crossed the seas. He meekly succumbed to what Taty had suggested earlier—mashed potatoes, green salad and plain rice.

KK ordered for a Vodka Martini, shaken not stirred, and thought that Taty would get impressed with the James Bond in him. As if to give a poke, Taty ordered her cocktail, Agent Orange. KK, who always had airs about having a high 'capacity' for drinks, in order to impress the girl, started gobbling in drinks one after the other. In India, unfortunately, manliness in measured by the number of drinks one can have and still appear to be normal, which is called ‘capacity’. More your ‘capacity’, the manlier you are and people look at you with awe.

But the Russian variant of the Vodka Martini was different and very strong in terms of alcohol content, considering the cold climate and the kind and quantity of red meat they consume. In short, within a couple of drinks, KK’s condition was much similar to what he was eating—mashed potatoes. The girl sensed it easily, with her vast experience with such idiotic males. She was waiting till KK’s masked serenity would fizzle out, and eventually it did.

It was easy for the gigantic Russian girl to carry the almost deadwood like KK to his room. KK, even is his inebriation, was enjoying the soft touch of the girl, which did not go unnoticed by her. By the time they came out of the elevator, she managed to get KK to kiss her. And all the while, she was observing the growing bulge on his crotch. Once they entered the room, things exploded literally, with the Indian showing his rapacity for the white skin. The lady had set the camera on, which was well concealed inside the button of her top, after having hanged it on the nearby dressing table.

It didn’t take much time for KK to start snoring after having ejected out the last few drops of energy left with him. The lady gave the sleeping brown-skinned man a disgusting look, quickly took a wash, put her clothes on and walked away leaving the door open.

Chapter 22

Ram's next challenge was to build a new team to carry out this new stream of business. Not only the Government or his chairperson, but the whole world was looking at this venture. Some of them were inquisitive to see whether India can replicate its success in space, in the deep waters too. But most of them were naysayers, especially the vested interests who wanted this venture to fail.

KK was not a natural choice for Ram, since he hated drunkards. For Ram, Shikhar was the choice to head the division. But he was not amused when a recommendation came from one of the Government under-secretaries, saying KK was a better person to handle the defence corridors. Knowing Shikhar as a straightforward and loyal executive, Ram had thought of him as his extended arm. But KK, with a mind of his own, could try some creativity on the job. Ram was sceptical of trying anybody who may try anything new on this highly critical project. But the orders of the government couldn't be ignored and as a new CEO, Ram also had his limitations. After all, Ram was yet to have his networking done in the corridors of power. Would KK help him do that? He decided to give the benefit of doubt to KK.

As usual, the Northern Indian group in Waveproof was taken aback at Shikhar's rejection. There were already murmurs in the company when Ram was declared as the successor of Grewal. The popular joke doing the rounds was that the company name was going to change to 'Saravana Bhavan', a famous Chennai restaurant. Another one mocked asking everyone to try practice eating *idli and vada*. The north-south divide always came out in the open whenever a south Indian was to take over the reins. It reminisced the plight of the erstwhile Prime Minister of India, P.V. Narasimha Rao, who was played down as the silent prime minister or the *Mouni Baba* (*Silent Saint*). The truth was that PVN was the best Prime Minister India ever had, who turned a bankrupt country into a global power in the making, what it is today. He was a genius who knew eight languages and excelled in any foreign meetings.

KK, as usual, brought in his coterie. Needless to say, Bala's name figured high on the list. Soon KK had his gang shift base to Mumbai. What was surprising was Fernando Coutinho also opened his branch in Chembur, as a token of his everlasting friendship with KK. The infamous Hyderabadgang slowly made one of the dance bars in Colaba as their den.

The mysterious man in a white t-shirt and blue denims, who was following KK whenever he was in Mumbai was also keeping a tab on him with his contacts in Hyderabad. Hence, he was well aware of KK's friend circle, and had a special inkling for Fernando Coutinho, when he shifted to Mumbai. Predictably, this man made it a habit to visit the Colaba dance bar, Blue Ecstasy, whenever he thought appropriate. His visits were not necessary once he won over a bartender, Mr. Freddy, and converted him into his informer.

Chapter 23

The strategy of diversifying into submarines and thereby reaping a new set of vendors worked wonders for Waveproof over a period of 4-5 years. The submarines were delivered one by one to the utmost satisfaction of the Indian government and also bringing relief to the straining IndoRussian relations because of the new world order. India's waters, which were under threat from the resurgent Chinese strategy of 'string of pearls', seemed to be much more secure after these submarines were added to the arsenal.

Commander Abdul Latif was one of those Russiatrained operators of the Submarine. In all, thirty Indians were trained to operate this high technology submarine at an undisclosed location in the Arctic seas. These were the most challenging sailing conditions where ice blocks and extremely cold temperatures added to the woes of a water that had varying density as per the proximity of icebergs. Abdul Latif was thinking of the famous book, 'Ice Station Zebra', by the legendary writer Alistair Maclean, when he was going through this tough training. The book narrates the struggle a British-American team of naval officers had to undergo to thwart a Soviet game plan of dominating the Arctic region. What shocked the British-Americans was the handiwork of a fellow British who happened to be a spy of the Soviets.

The Russians were told by the Indian defence to train their guys in simulated conditions of the South China Sea.

This is where the Indians can hold the Chinese to their hooks if conditions worsened between them. The Chinese energy supplies were routed through the newly built China-Pakistan Economic Corridor from Balochistan to China's South-West point, bordering Pakistan. This corridor, which was within striking distance from Indian military bases in Western India, always gave sleepless nights to China. Hence, South China Sea was an effective alternative when it came to Indian challenge. On the contrary, the tensions with Japan and Korea made it necessary for China to keep the Pakistan option also alive.

The month-long training was initially a torture for the Indians. They could not even imagine the amount of cold. They would sarcastically say that their penis has shrunk and recoiled inside due to the acute cold, and therefore the Indian government has made them women. But as the days passed, they got used to the cold, as they mimicked their Russian counterparts by gulping Vodka during training hours to beat the biting freeze.

So, when the training came to an end, they no more saw it as an ordeal, but as a lifetime experience to cherish. But the cherry on the cake was the party that was thrown open to them at the culmination of training in St. Petersburg. If booze, bite and bass was all common to any party, what was uncommon to this party were the waitresses, all scantily clad and ready for anything. While most of them made merry of this once-in-a-lifetime opportunity, Commander Latif stood to his reputation of his royal heritage. Scion of the Malabar royal family, he kept away from wine and women. His integrity and sharpness always drew ire of the fellow officers, but brilliance seldom got overshadowed by awe.

So, when the crew of thirty returned back home, the Indian Navy had received a secret recommendation list from the Russians, where Commander Latif stood as the most reliable officer.

Chapter 24

KK was not a pushover when it came to political connections, something which came as a pleasant surprise to Ram. Soon after the bonhomie subsequent to the successful return of the Russia-trained naval officers, the Indian government came out with an order for the next variety of Rosmarine submarines called the Stingray, the latest in the industry. The Russian gesture to share the most advanced submarine technology in the world soon caught the attention of the world. The envied American and Chinese media cried foul, saying the Lioness' boobs did the trick with the Russian premier. Trolls across Twitter called out to the American and Chinese presidents to grow breasts, so that they too could get the best of technology from the horny Russian supremo.

As expected, there was the usual push and pull in the high corridors of the defence ministry to grab this prestigious order. The state-owned manufacturers staked their claim for the most secretive projects but it was something the international marine industry looked into with envy. Given the security risks involved in the project, giving it to a private company was ruled out. The competition was limited only to the three state-owned manufacturers.

Seeing the clear mandate from the government, all the private contenders lost hope and stayed away. But not KK.

Stingray had the technical specifications that made it the only submarine to undergo the hardest of aquatic conditions, namely the salinity and the related high density and corrosion. It was designed to withstand the uncertainties of Halocline. Halocline is the immediate layer under the sea surface that has the maximum variation of salinity and causes ambiguity in the performance of the vessel. This creates accidents, inability to forecast the location of the submarine which was a difficulty when it came to plan a strike on the enemy.

It was difficult to simulate this condition during testing since the surface salinity did not vary much, unless when compared during peak summer to peak rainy season. Halocline but shows a 3-4% variation between short distances of a few nautical miles.

The shipyard of Waveproof had this added advantage of being near a river mouth. With a plethora of dams upstream, and an acute fight between the states made it mandatory for these dams to release water into the river at frequent intervals. This sudden dilution of sea water created the same variation as found inside a Halocline layer.

This peculiarity of Stingray and the unique sea conditions it required for testing were something that the ministry had not taken note off. The Russian sea conditions near the Arctic had this density variation built in because of the presence of ice and its frequent melting during day time. Since this is not a special condition as far as Russians are concerned, they did not mention it in their guidelines either. It required years of wisdom and expertise that Ram had possessed throughout his career to highlight this loophole, which if not addressed would cause the failure of submarines during operation.

This piece of information was enough for KK to create havoc in the Lutyens. KK, who deliberately leaked the information to the opposition, managed to create a standstill in the parliament. There was a clarion call from the opposition and media that the government should step down for this laxity.

Soon the Lioness had to make a statement that this special sea condition will be a deciding factor for the ordering. Obviously, the only ship manufacturer in India who satisfied this condition was Waveproof. KK passed with flying colours when the government announced its decision to award the contract to Waveproof on a nomination basis, avoiding all tendering activities. It was for the first time that government's decision to award the contract on a private party was welcomed whole-heartedly by everyone including the opposition. It was party time in Waveproof, and KK was the talk of the town.

Chapter 25

Shikhar, however, was upset about Waveproof bagging this prestigious and much envied order. With just one knock-out punch, KK dethroned his arch rival putting rest to the speculation about who was the second-in-command in Waveproof. Even Ram felt KK was breathing right over his shoulder, from the way he started talking with confidence and pomp during the senior management meetings. Though the idea of pitching in the concerns about the Halocline layer was that of Ram, KK simply walked away with credit. The only solace for Ram was the hatred Namy carried for KK, for he was a drunkard.

KK, after having officially promoted to be the president of the operations, started stepping up his activities. He considered going to 'Blue Ecstasy' below his status. He started frequenting 'The Maratha', a leading five-star hotel overlooking the Queen's necklace in the plush Marine Drive area of Mumbai. KK's brand new Audi Q7 was a regular in the parking area, his chauffeur cursing his master for his haphazard lifestyle that spoiled the poor man's family time.

KK used to drink until wee hours, putting all his colleagues in trouble. Many colleagues hanged around with him for promotions and other favours. He was a benevolent dictator and helped whoever were in his good books. One

Vadassery Thaiparambil rakesh

good thing about KK was that he might go back home in the odd hours, but always made sure to be present in the office in time. This made his colleagues crib. Many of them suffered from blood pressure, cholesterol, lack of libido, erectile dysfunction, obesity, accidents and divorces. All of this because of continuous drinking, lack of sleep, outside food, and disturbance in family life. His drivers never stayed for more than six months, making him sometimes drive himself after the drinks.

It was one such late night party after which he had to drive himself back. It was a relatively long drive from Marine Drive towards Carmichael Road near the famous Mahalakshmi temple. It was nearing 4 in the morning and the full moon was getting ready to take a plunge into the warm sea. KK, who was yet to finish his honeymoon with the new Audi Q7, was excited at the light breeze, empty roads and above all the urge to step up on the gas. The German machine roared in applause of its freedom to excel. The car zoomed above 150 kmph and KK felt like Emperor Shivaji zooming on his horse across the heart of India. And suddenly like Aurangazeb, a black Land Rover (LR) crisscrossed in front of Haji Ali. If not for the finesse of German engineering, the cars would have crashed to shambles. The Audi with its tyre width and AntiBraking System (ABS) managed to brush past the BritishIndian icon. The sparks created during the caress brought KK back to his senses. And before he could think of reacting, a well-built man came out of the LR and asked him to come out. The LR had blocked the way, hence driving out was not an option. KK, though terrified to the hilt, decided to play good by coming out and saying sorry. Suddenly, he felt strong arms come around him. One pair tied a black cloth over his eyes, the other pair pulled his arms behind and tied his wrists together. A third pair of strong arms lifted him up like a baby and threw him inside their car. Soon both the vehicles raced away back into the concrete jungles of Mumbai, leaving no trace of what had happened.

The daily morning meeting of the senior management at Waveproof, which was hitherto a weekly meeting called up daily in the wake of the new Stingray orders, was conspicuous with the absence of KK. It was a chance for Shikhar to rake up the issue of self-discipline needed for the organization to execute such an order of national importance. Given the high security and scrutiny needed for the job, Shikhar wanted a daily closing meeting in the late evening, purposefully suggested to scuttle the get-togethers of rival camp. In the absence of KK, the management agreed to this proposal unanimously.

Chapter 26

KK opened his eyes with great difficulty. Last night's torture, both mental and physical, had taken its toll. He could vaguely remember what happened last night. He was taken captive inside an old gear manufacturing unit, only an hour's drive from the heart of Mumbai. The abandoned factory was a perfect camouflage for the abductors. A pleasant smell of baked dough was coming from an adjoining factory. The abductors had planned out very well, since the inside of the factory was having all the amenities, like a plush office, an internet connection, a small bar, and a place for overnight stay. KK was asked about the present defence orders and whenever they felt he was not telling the truth, they applied ice on his private parts. KK showed lot of determination despite the pain he had to undergo.

But he was startled to see photographs and videos of his escapade in St. Petersburg. Taty, the girl who got KK laid, had a camera installed on her shirt and had shot the sex act in all its intensity. KK was thrilled to see the passionate act and was wondering how Vodka made him more virile. But soon the reality sunk in and he started sulking.

There were three men altogether, taking turns in questioning him. They made him strip and he had to sit on a toilet chair. With his hands tied behind and legs chained to a nearby pole, KK realized that what was to come won't be very pleasant. As expected, it was horrible. They whipped his balls from under the chair with a thick rope. KK's eyeballs popped out in writhing pain each time the rope caressed the testicles. He called out for help in desperation.

The three guys phoned up someone and informed about his meek surrender. The phone was kept near him and KK was asked to talk. KK was truthful when he told that, at present, there was not much he knew, but as and when he will come to know he promised to spill the beans. Though KK at that time told this to avoid any further torture, that statement was welcomed whole-heartedly by the group. He was given a strict warning that any attempt to seek police or government help would be suicidal. The whole episode with Taty, they said, would be distributed all across to tarnish not only KK's image, but to put the whole lot of Indian professionals traveling to foreign shores in a poor light.

The smug that KK was, he had no problems in agreeing to the deal. They made KK sign a paper, and after having got it signed, read it out to him. It was a confession statement to the nation. It said he had leaked out the nation's important defence secrets for sexual favours. It was followed by a suicide note, saying that he was shooting himself as a penance to the irreparable damage he had done to the nation and its people.

Any non-concurrence to the deal, and what awaited him was not only death but the ignominy of being a traitor and a sex maniac, and also the perennial stain it would bring to his family, his community and his ilk.

Chapter 27

"Why the sun has to set
When the eyes are already wet
Why souls have to depart
When life always sets us apart
Why hearts stop to beat
When heartless roam the street
Why eyes stop to flutter
When justice always stutter
Why anyone need a foe
When love always end in a woe"

Namy had etched this poem not only in her office, but very much in her heart. A poem written by her husband Jeremy. Since the couple had no children of their own, Jeremy decided to have a pet dog. He loved it so much that at times Namy was jealous of this dog. But looking at the happiness and contentment on Jeremy's face, she toned down her displeasure. Her inability to bear a child always haunted her and at times made her scoff at people around her without a reason. Jeremy had written those lines out of acute grief when the dog died of old age.

But that Monday morning, the daily meeting saw an unusual burst of anger from Namy. And this time it was on the poster boy, KK. KK's demeanour and the newfound assertiveness about the Stingray order, didn't go well with her. Moreover, she hated men who had a dominating trait, something to do with her struggle in this male dominated society. One of the main reasons she was comfortable with Ram was because of his courteous way of carrying himself. Whenever she saw Ram, it reminded her of the cricketer Rahul Dravid, who was an epitome of gentlemanly mannerisms. At times, seeing Ram's non-aggressive approach, she wondered how he had managed his people. But the track record told Namy that there was something more to Ram than what met the eye.

It was really a test of temperament for KK, who struggled to contain his disdain for Namy. KK, being a misogynist, considered women nothing more than a sex object. In his typical fashion, KK sat nonchalantly without a frown on his face. People who knew KK were amused at his new-found temperament.

Ram's timely interference saved the day for both Namy and KK. Ram was particularly critical of the group for concentrating only on the project execution and not focussing on technology adoption. He was very concerned that the Indian companies unlike their Chinese counterparts were dumb heads when it came to technology adoption. The Chinese, who partnered with Japanese or European companies, were smartly owning up technology and after a maximum of ten years of partnership used to dump the foreign partner. They would make an improvisation on the acquired technology and patent it, making it unnecessary to pay royalties to the foreign partner. Indians, in their typical subservient mind-set, would heed the lines of the foreign partner and keep the partnership for twenty–thirty years. Their dependence on the partner and, therefore, on foreigners remained and the country was always at the mercy of these foreigners.

Ram hijacked the meeting with his action plan for technology acquisition. He had already picked the brightest design brains in his company and brought in a retired design chief, Mr. Sobu Sam, from the Indian space agency, ISRO, to oversee the technology acquisition plan. Ram's diktat for Sobu was clear. Five years was what Sobu got to acquire the whole technology of Stingray. After five years, Waveproof should be able to cater to the nation's submarine needs. Ram was waiting to see the day when, for the security of the Tricolour, the nation need not beg for any foreign support.

Chapter 28

Stingray, as expected, dominated the mental space of everyone in Waveproof. Slowly but surely the well-earned progress in capturing the foreign accounts under Ram, was dying down. Ram was expecting this and was painfully observing that the company was unnecessarily euphoric about one single order, putting its bread-and-butter business in jeopardy.

It was during one of those morning meetings that an otherwise calm and cool Ram exploded. And he had come with all the data, proving it to the people who mattered that it was a pre-determined outburst. He showed what the ROI and cash flows from the Stingray deal were. Though the project came at a decent margin, the over importance and resource allocation to it was taking a toll elsewhere, which would eventually cause the company to sink. Notwithstanding the good probability of repeat orders and the consistent stream of revenue they may generate in the future, Ram wanted to highlight that the competition was also gearing up to have a go for the next Stingray orders. A couple of them zeroed in on the natural halocline river mouths to put up shipyards dedicated to cater to the submarine manufacturing. Such was the potential of the business.

Ram also had brought the details of the routine business slowdown. He had charted how the business would progress if he had his way in propelling the foreign business. The consistent profitability that the business ensured was far outweighing the projected profits from the Stingray deals.

Ram's sudden adrenaline rush had its desired effect. Namy declared in that meeting that she wanted the Stingray project to be declared a separate Strategic Business Unit (SBU), and a team be earmarked and kept separate. The SBU head should be named by Ram, and his reporting to Ram would be only through a monthly meeting. That would give enough breathing space for everyone to focus on mainstream orders and ensure sustenance.

Once the meeting was over, another canvassing war started between KK and Shikhar for the coveted post of SBU head. For KK, this was literally a case of life and death, since a failure to satisfy his blackmailers meant instant death and disgrace. Hence KK was determined to grab this post by hook or crook. Shikhar saw this as the greatest opportunity to levelup with KK, the battle he thought he was losing out.

Knowing that Ram was a forthright and just person, Shikhar decided to work on Ram. He stressed upon the need for a hands-on technical person like him to lead the show, as execution and not business development is the key to success. Knowing that the contacts in the ministry was not a permanent advantage for KK, since the ministry may change anytime, Shikhar conveyed emphatically that business development can be ensured only through proven execution experience and servicing and not through high contacts.

KK, knowing Ram's and Namy's aversion for him, thought of doing something different. He brought to Ram's notice the limited value addition he could bring in the mainstream business. Ram being the champion of international business development, KK used the analogy of a moon on a sunny sky to drive home the point that he could do nothing substantial while Ram is there. He also subtly indicated that Ram being the champion salesman, he needs to be supplemented by a strong service person like Shikhar, to create an impact in the foreign markets. It was a veiled attempt to say that Ram and Shikhar should stay put with the international business.

KK was in no mood to leave any stone unturned. He even went to the ministry to do some liaising. Soon the ministry came out with a committee to steer private partnership in defence manufacturing, where KK's name appeared prominently. The only name from Waveproof in the ministry of defence's committee to develop private partnership. Shikhar once again had to bite the dust, when Ram had no option but to announce KK as the SBU head in the next monthly meeting.

Chapter 29

It was a novel experience for Waveproof to build a ship with foreigners dominating the show. The prerequisite for the job was providing a full-fledged facility for the Russians to put base. Two towers in Mumbai's upmarket Hiranandani Towers in Thane were booked fully for the Russians. The additional facilities included bar, sauna, spa, swimming pool, gymnasium and a full-fledged gaming centre with the latest gizmos.

Unlike India, the Russian work force was dominated by women, even the supposedly tough jobs like specialised welders. Most of the decision makers too were ladies. Coming from a male dominated society, it was initially difficult for the Indians to digest this. But later on, the work cultures merged and work progressed smoothly. And as expected Indians were behind the Russian girls more for their beauty than their technical acumen.

Sobu had a tough time getting his men to concentrate on technology and not on cleavage. But the genius of Sobu made it mandatory for his people to absorb the technology, otherwise they were ruthlessly transferred to other sections. Hence, to make sure they continued to be in proximity to the girls, his people made extra efforts to gulp in the technology. Ram's judgment about Sobu was one hundred percent right and technology was being absorbed, with the Russians least expecting it at such a speed. Wherever objections in handing over the drawings and specifications came, it was well taken care of with Vodka for men and expensive gifts like diamonds and jewellery for women.

Maria Semenova was the design head of Rosemarine. A well-built woman in her early forties, she had the looks of a Greek goddess. A divorcee and a single mother, she was wedded to her job, and gave the impression that nothing else mattered in her life. Stingray was her pet project, which fetched her many an accolade from the government and the defence equipment fraternity. And she stood like the Himalayas between Sobu and his plans to make India self-reliant when it came to submarine technology.

Hence the next challenge for Ram's astute brain was to find a way to tackle this Russian woman. Vodka and women worked with Russian men; he did not have a clue what could work with this aging beauty. But not after he met Commander Latif.

Commander Latif, who came out with flying colours after the naval training in St. Petersburg, was sent by the navy as an inspector to Waveproof. He was accorded with the apparent purpose of ensuring quality from the point of view of the ultimate user. But it was the navy's way of trying to know what all was going on. Latif, with his princely looks and sharp acumen, soon became a part and parcel of the Waveproof execution team. He took special interest to oversee the technology transfer and the Indians' ability to digest what was transferred. But soon he discovered that what was transferred as technology was just peanuts and with such meagre details that it would take the nation another hundred years to indigenize the design.

Latif saw Maria Semenova as the main culprit standing in the way of his nation's best interests. He, as a proud Indian naval officer, could not stand the sight of anyone who was against his nation. But confronting the Russian was of no use, as she could find a hundred ways to say no to him. But Latif knew of only one thing that he was sure that the lady would not say no to him for. And he decided to do exactly that.

Chapter 30

Within a span of 24 months the first batch of Stingrays was handed over to the Indian Navy with much fanfare. The defence minister was found proudly flaunting his presence in the absence of his boss, the Lioness. KK was competing with him to steal the limelight, though Namy and Ram were looming large, as for the general public and the media, Waveproof was all about this duo of Namy and Ram.

And in all these 24 months, KK kept on meeting his tormentors and passed on vital information like drawings, control systems, and other key features like tracking options and apparent loopholes. Not even once did he feel remorse or even thought about reporting this to either his management or the police. This was despite the clout he enjoyed in the ministry and the government. It was not that he was overly perturbed by the blackmails. In reality, he didn't even care a damn about the country.

Attending the handing over ceremony were a bunch of naval officers who accompanied the Naval Chief who in turn was flanking the defence minister all the while. One officer stood out with his extremely handsome looks. Not very far, he could see the lady who had given him a rose, one that he was carrying in the pocket of his jacket right now. Her wet eyes signalled her departure from India after having completed a successful stint of kick-starting the first major submarine deal between Russia and India, bolstering further the already concrete ties between two allies. But only Latif and Maria knew the real reason behind those tears.

Sobu was given a big rise as Ram's plan of imbibing the technology fully bore fruit. Little did Sobu know what facilitated a smooth technology transfer, much better than what was usually expected from Russians.

That month 'Business India', India's foremost business magazine, carried out a frontpage article on Waveproof, describing it as the emerging blue-chip company of India. Ram was hailed as the CEO to look for, as he had turned the tides for the company. He was duly credited for putting the eggs in two baskets, one the burgeoning domestic defence market and the other, time tested and reliable international freight market. While the former can give a handsome bottom-line, the latter gave the much-needed stable top-line. And he delivered on both fronts.

The article also carried an interview with both Namy and Ram, wherein both showered praise on each other. Namy was particularly generous in praising Ram, singularly giving him the credit for the upswing of the international business. The core team of KK, Shikhar and also the key members like Bala got either mentioned or were featured with a photograph. In short, it was party time in Waveproof.

Chapter 31

Stingray caused quite a furore in the Asian continent. The maverick and xenophobic President of the USA was in no mood to succumb to Pakistan's cry for balancing power in the Indian sub-continent. The US President was more worried about his country losing economic dominance to China, than meddle in the petty quarrels elsewhere. The Chinese equivalent of Stingray was a laughingstock the world over. To quote a US General who famously said, "The Chinese vessels need no US battle ships to stop them, they trip even over paper waste." The Chinese alternative was not even acceptable to their greatest ally—Pakistan.

The bottom line in the foreign affairs department in Delhi was, "In matters of foreign affairs, the Lioness has always had her way". And Pakistan was always at the receiving end of this, since one by one the world nations started throwing their weight behind India, partly because of India's huge market potential.

With Stingray in the stable, the Indian Navy was back in the reckoning in the Indian Ocean, putting a remarkable challenge to the Chinese 'string of pearls' strategy. Though the Chinese loomed large with sheer numbers, when it came to quality, the world had its own doubts. That was the solace Indians had, though they knew it was a lost battle when it came to numbers.

South China Sea was boiling with territorial tensions. The North Korean dictator, with tacit support from China, was giving sleepless nights to all its neighbours, especially their brothers South Korea and also Japan. It was at this time that the maverick American president decided to flex his muscles.

The U.S. 7th Fleet (C7F) operates as the largest of the U.S. Navy's numbered fleets. At any given time, there are 70-80 ships and submarines, 140 aircraft and approximately 40,000 sailors and marines in the region of its deployment. It was widely believed that apart from a couple of world's leading countries, none of the nations can withstand the power of a 7th fleet. In short, USA requires only this fleet to defeat almost anybody in the world.

What irked the world in general and the Americans in particular was when the North Koreans built something that was nicknamed 'Porcupine'. It was a battery of, 'ready to launch' nuclear missiles on the border with South Koreans. North Korea's premier, who was nothing but a Chinese puppet, went to the press to talk about the 'Porcupine', mocking the world's most powerful man. He described it as the thorny throne that was reserved for the President's arse.

But South China Sea was strategically very important for China as its energy supplies came through this sea. An American presence in this sea meant being at their mercy. It was at this juncture that they supplied a huge array of submarines to North Korea. These subs were the ones the world poo-pooed highlighting the quality issues. North Korea was supposed to scuttle the seemingly formidable 7th fleet with these subs.

It was also an opportunity for the Chinese to test their subs in actual war conditions at somebody else's expense. Soon the grandeur of the 7th fleet started sailing towards the

Korean peninsula defying the warnings from North Korea as well as China. China even involved its friend-in-need Russia to douse down the flaring tensions. But a maverick is always a maverick. The President was more worried about a rogue nation challenging the might of the world's only superpower.

Chapter 32

The world was face to face with an impending nuclear war. Despite the cries and calls for peace, there was nothing stopping the American juggernaut. Its war ships had all the sophisticated arrangements to detect and destroy all the torpedoes and submarines. The latest satellite technology, called the 'eagle-eye', helped the Americans scan everything inside the sea up to a depth of 100 meters. This was synchronised with the armour in the ships.

Once the underwater objects were detected to have metallic content, the special torpedoes synchronised with the target through the satellite, and pursued till the target was destroyed. It was impossible to touch this fleet, war experts the world over gave their verdict.

And soon, sighting the North Korean submarines, these special torpedoes that could be launched automatically on detection of the target, were launched one by one. There was rejoice in the American camp each time they sensed the explosions. "Chinese subs are getting killed like moths", tweeted the American Navy's official twitter handle.

The world went gaga about the American technological prowess, once again being sarcastic at anything made in China. It was then that it struck the American fleet's admiral. Why on earth are the Koreans allowing their subs to be destroyed like this, when they knew that the subs do not have a chance of survival? He decided to stop the satellites from controlling the detonation of torpedoes. He ordered to allow the subs to come closer to their ships

The Korean subs came like zombies and travelled without any particular intention. After having observed for a while, the Americans decided to capture one of them. After having captured that sub, it gave one of the greatest shocks and a realisation that the world's greatest military force had been taken for an underwater ride.

The sub had nothing but a propeller and a programmed path. They were all dummy submarines made to fool the American satellites. Americans realised the damage when they saw the number of torpedoes wasted in the process, making them short of torpedoes if the real submarines were to come.

The Koreans had sensors attached to these dummies, and once they realised that the cat is out of the bag, they quickly swung into action. While the Americans were still taking time to digest the damage, the real Korean submarines which looked exactly like the dummies entered under the fleet. Before the Americans could realise, the subs started sinking the ships one by one. The Chinese torpedoes literally made mincemeat of the huge ships, pulling them down like an underwater demon.

Soon, it started looking like the Vietnam War. Once again, a formidable force started succumbing to the sharp acumen of a lesser force.

Chapter 33

The retreat of the 7th fleet did not mean the world's superpower was on its knees. It was rather like a recoiling snake that would strike back with all its venom. And the Chinese knew this better than anyone else. It then became imperative for China to avoid this retribution from the world's mightiest power.

Flanking is a strategy used by marketers worldwide, but they had borrowed it from the various wars that were fought in history. The best example of flanking was seen in the second world war on what later came to be known as the D-Day.

"Planning for the operation began in 1943. In the months leading up to the invasion, the Allies conducted a substantial military deception, codenamed Operation Bodyguard, to mislead the Germans as to the date and location of the main Allied landings. The weather on D-Day was far from ideal, but postponing would have meant a delay of at least two weeks, as the invasion planners had requirements for the phase of the moon, the tides, and the time of day that meant only a few days in each month were deemed suitable. Adolf Hitler placed German Field Marshal Erwin Rommel in command of German forces and of developing fortifications along the Atlantic Wall in anticipation of an Allied invasion. The Allies kept on flanking from different parts; the Germans could never guess which the real attack was. And after all the Normandy landings happened, Germans thought it was a diversionary tactic and did not take it seriously."

The Chinese decided to take a leaf out of the Allies' book. In fact, they were seething for revenge after they lost out to the Indians a few years back after they had invaded a strategic island in the Indian Ocean. The Indians' meticulous planning and the local support helped them thwart the Chinese with minimal casualties on both ends. The Tape island that was torn by the civil war was invaded by the Chinese then to meet their nuclear needs. The island, which was a rich source of thorium, catered well into the Chinese ambitions of relying solely on nuclear power, having depleted the coal reserves. Also, importing coal was a risky proposition since they had to depend on the uncertain sea routes and also on American allies like Australia and Indonesia. Ever since their plan was foiled by the Indians, they were looking for an opportunity to get back. And this was their opportunity to kill two birds with one stone.

Chapter 34

The Andaman and Nicobar Islands are about a thousand kilometres away from the nearest Indian mainland city of Chennai. The archipelago was strategic as far as India was concerned. Port Blair was the capital city and home to the local base of India's three forces. The place was mostly considered as a holiday destination as nothing except tourism worked there. Like the more famous Indian destination of Goa, the name Andamans evoked the feeling of holidaying.

It was another cosy day for the forces in the island. Commander Abdul Latif had struggled the last six months since he joined duty in Port Blair to take out the tardiness from his people. He was very particular when it came to naval drills and the daily routine of alertness to be maintained by armed forces. He always believed that the enemy was always on the prowl like the proverbial Bengal tiger in the Sundarbans. And it attacked at a time when the prey least expected.

Commander Latif, though an atheist, was somehow seeing all bad omens that day. He had a flat tyre when he was about to mount his jeep. The seagulls seemed to be restless as he was driving. There was a beggar he always made sure to stop by and pay alms to. That day, however, she was nowhere to be seen and, as if reading his probing eyes, the nearby hawker conveyed the news of the elderly and hapless lady's accidental death.

It was with an uneasy and turbulent mind, that too without an apparent reason, that this astute officer of the Indian Navy took command of the Stingray submarine named INS Chamunda, for its usual surveillance operations. The trip would normally last around ten days. Being the Russia-trained officer, he had a bunch of officers with him as trainees.

The ten-day routine did not necessarily mean that they followed the beaten down paths under the sea, though normally they avoided criss-crossing the trade route to avoid unwarranted mishaps. This time they ventured out in a new direction towards the eastern waters. The Stingray was by this time the pet of Commander Latif. He fell in love with its manoeuvrability, speed and control. The firing prowess was the icing on the cake. He sincerely felt that the Indian Navy finally had a winner in her hands.

The eastern waters had a lot many uninhabited small islands. Latif's idea was to use these islands to train his people to fire dummy missiles. The islands posed as imaginary battle ships of the enemy, bearing the brunt of highly skilled Indian officers. INS Chamunda that day reminded of the great warrior Arjun, whose arrows hit the enemy always on the bull's eye. Missiles sprung up like dolphins from under the water and pounced on each of the islands in the vicinity.

Latif was on his usual probe with the periscope to locate another nearby island when he saw it. From a distance, he doubted whether it was a tsunami roaring towards them. But the sea around him was very normal, except for the small turbulence created by them. Another clear look and he had to rub his eyes in disbelief.

Chapter 35

The Andaman and Nicobar Islands were a tactical base for the Indians. What worried the Chinese more was the rising bonhomie of Indians with the Americans. They suspected the islands were being used by the USA as a base under the garb of Indian forces. This endangered the Chinese energy supplies that were routed very near to those islands. So, it was a perfect case of killing two birds with a single shot for the Chinese.

The Chinese fleet that used to be docked at the Pakistan port of Gwadar, was a quid pro quo by China for having allowed to build an economic corridor. It was in the wake of an impending war in South China Sea that the Chinese decided to move this fleet towards the disturbed area. The fleet was nicknamed Fa Hien, in memory of the Great Chinese traveller who helped invent the silk route. It was a veiled reference to its intentions on India as Fa Hien had taken away many Buddhist texts from India, eventually resulting in the waning of Buddhism in India and its waxing in China.

It was when the fleet was near the Philippines that the idea of flanking struck the Chinese. The fleet took a U turn and headed for the Andamans. They were not expecting a fight, since earlier the fleet could move without any hassles through the international trade route which was very near to Andamans. If the Americans had a base there, they would have created obstacles for sure.

It was a moment of perplexity for Latif, for he went totally blank about what to do next. A small submarine against the might of Fa Hien, was like David against Goliath. Latif's mind was running like a hare. He turned around the submarine and was at full throttle back to the naval base lest the war ships detect the submarine. His SOS call went through to the naval headquarters creating a shudder throughout the country's echelons of power.

For the Chinese, it was literally a case of catching the enemy sleeping. The Indians never expected such an attack when a nuclear war was about to get triggered in the South China Sea. But the brave hearts posted at Andamans were not the ones who would bite the dust so easily. They had an array of three destroyers, one submarine and a dozen gun boats. The naval air station had a couple of Rafales and four attack helicopters. All this against the impending Chinese might of an aircraft carrier with twenty five latest Sukhoi-35, three battle ships and at least a dozen submarines. To add to that, the fleet was flanked by four destroyers.

Fa Hien was a hundred nautical miles away from Port Blair, when the decision to not attack came from the Indian mainland.

Chapter 36

The Chinese expectation to find American forces in the island failed miserably. Unlike what they thought, Indian soil was fully sovereign and no foreign powers had any stake there. But this was bad news for them, since their strategy of opening a war front much away from South China Sea would fail.

Having put base at the Andamans and having seen that the island had enough resources, they decided to stay put. The world was stunned to see the Chinese aggression on Indian soil. But they were more shocked to see the meek Indian reaction.

Now with the international trader route a stone's throw away from its newly acquired base, the Chinese embargoed the route. They chose which ship should pass through and which one had to be turned back/confiscated. The whole far-east economy was thrown topsy-turvy since all of them depended on Western Asia for their energy supplies. These countries would have collapsed totally but for the emergency supplies organized by the NATO countries through the Pacific.

This embargo effectively worked as a counterweight to western aggressions in the South China Sea. The small countries like South Korea, Japan, Philippines, and Indonesia who were clamouring for western intervention to clamp North Korea and China, mellowed down their rhetoric in the wake of soaring commodity prices fuelled by a huge energy bill and a public outcry for peace.

Naturally the vested interests started blaming India's meek surrender as the root cause to their problems thus instigating Indians. Indians were portrayed as ostriches in the international media. A particular neighbouring country of India was very interested to fan the flames and fish in the troubled waters. Indians were pictured as eunuchs to further poke the emotions across the border.

The mercurial Indian leader, the Lioness as she was called, played down all the vitriolic clamours aimed at her. She was clear that the Indian restraint had rescued the world from an impending nuclear war in South China Sea. And the world slowly but surely acknowledged that. In fact, the embargo had convinced the American cronies in South China Sea that they were more vulnerable than they thought. "Rhetoric is easy but reality is tough", her words were marked by the world as historic.

Soon the tension diffused in South China Sea and the 7th fleet took a retreat to Australian shores signalling a strategic victory for the Chinese. The American retreat was also a signal for the Chinese to leave the Andamans and restore the trade route to bring normalcy.

Chapter 37

Months passed by and this time the sarcastic caricatures that flashed across the world were that of the proverbial Arab and the camel—the camel occupying its master's tent and displacing him to the cold desert sands.

The world was more or less convinced about the tacit understanding the two Asian super powers had, to prevent a western incursion in Asia. And it was a slap on the face of all western powers and media, who always enjoyed at fingering on the miseries of third world. Here were two countries who cooperated to avoid tensions across the globe and kept out a bully at arm's length. Peace lovers across the globe applauded this astuteness of the Lioness.

Soon the world accepted the Chinese accession of Andamans as a fait accompli and moved on. But the worries of over a billion people in India were not to cede. The opposition parties in India made a mockery of the Lioness for having parted with the Indian land to make peace for others. They also made merry of the general aversion the Indians had against the past Chinese aggressions in India, using it to ferment emotions against the Lioness. But the opposition was gullibly falling prey to the evil designs of a neighbouring country. The press, as usual focused on increasing their TRPs and made a mockery of government.

The public sentiment also rose to such a high fervour that it sent shivers down the spine of the government. The curse of a democratic government is the dilemma it faces on a daily basis. Neither could it reveal its strategic secrets to the citizens. Nor could it act based on public outcry, which in most cases was without knowing the full facts. Finally, it happened what normally happens in all hapless democracies. Playing to the galleries began.

It was with much pain that the Indians had to ask the Chinese to leave their territory. Chinese were dumbstruck with this kind of populism that they were never accustomed with. Being a communist country, China had no needs to become populist. But its decisions would be all the more conducive to people in the long run. In return to India's timely help, Chinese had crippled the nuclear dreams of a neighbouring nation that was always a thorn in the flesh for India. Chinese must have felt that India was not a democracy but a 'democrazy', looking at the foolishness its people were pushing its government to.

But soon it was time for the Indians to get startled. The Chinese bluntly refused to vacate the occupied islands. They were justified in their argument that it was well planned and agreed between the two countries. Going back on the commitment cannot be an option in such deals which are purely based on trust. But what do they know of public pressure in a democracy. They simply asked the Indians to suppress and if needed use brutal force to contain the people. This was reminiscent of what they did to their agitating students three-four decades back. But they could never understand the Indian ethos, wherein killing even animals are avoided. And in a democracy violence has a lasting effect, something that can bite you back even after decades.

Chapter 38

Commander Latif had taken the submarine to Barren Island, one of the islands in the archipelago. Barren Island was the only active volcano in South Asia. And it was indeed fuming that part of the year, apparently unhappy about the foreign presence.

Barren island, which was relatively uninhabited by both human beings and animals because of the frequent outburst of the volcano, was a perfect place to build a secret dwelling. Indian forces had built this place under the garb of a thickly vegetated hill slope adjoining the sea. The hill overhung into the sea giving enough depth of water ensuring necessary draft for the vessels to dock. It also helped the submarine lie submerged adjacent to the land.

The sea caved in to the land making the protrusion even more acute. And where the sea made its vertex, the hill had a natural grotto. This worked as an ambush that was not visible from either open sea or the land. The cavern had a battery of 'land to land' missiles that, if launched, could never miss the targets anywhere in the Andamans. The '*Vel*', that's what it was called, named after Lord Karthikeya's spear, had a hitting radius of 100 kilometres, but what made it ominous was the deadly accuracy. It worked on the satellite-controlled navigation systems, making it possible to hit moving objects like a ship. And unlike the heat seeking missiles, the *Vel* was not gullible, unless the satellite is wrong.

The secret mission personnel perennially placed at Barren islands was always ready for such a situation. The islands being a thousand kilometre away from the mainland was always susceptible to such acrimony. And the limited forces placed there were resourceful for staying alive for months without any supplementary supplies. This is knowing that they may have to lie in ambush since they wouldn't be able to take on a massive enemy offensive head-on. Neither the country could afford to put a full-fledged fleet for safe-guarding the island.

The special amphibious commandoes were trained for both land and water combats. There were twenty-five commandoes that were chosen from the best in country. And they were all at the command of arguably one of the finest navigators in India, Commander Latif.

Code named Operation Surasa, Commander Latif had chalked out his game plan meticulously. He was wanting to repeat the victory of Lord Hanuman over the sea-demoness Surasa. The *Ramayan* had all the ingredients of the David and Goliath story on how a small task force can destabilise a larger enemy. Twenty-five commandoes and a commander, could they make it happen?

Chapter 39

The erstwhile Indian naval base was no more in a recognisable form. The small destroyers that adorned the base had shifted back to India. The place was taken over by huge battle ships and its array of gun boats. The whole area was converted to a cantonment for Chinese forces. It looked like a Shanghai downtown, more than an Indian piece of land. Many Indians who were part of the local populace had left the place feeling uncomfortable with a foreign rule. But the few of them who decided to stay back, did it for a reason.

Latif had implants among these people staying there. At least a handful of people who stayed back at Port Blair were trained agents who understood everything connected with defence forces. It was from them that he came to know about more forces joining in through the now peaceful South China Sea. This was alarming since it went against the understanding between two countries. And instead of reducing the forces and planning to leave the territory back to Indians, this addition of forces seemed nefarious.

The Indian satellite, *'Sanjaya'*, had one of the best resolutions in this sector. It's said that an eagle can see a small fish under water from even a height of a few kilometres. This spy satellite was designed with the same philosophy. It was named after a *Mahabharat* character who could see what was happening in the war front sitting in the comforts of home. The *Sanjaya* satellite was an envy of the world since the height from which it operated was much more than what the other satellites operated from. This added height gave it a better view and it could encapsulate the world in a few snaps that too with an accuracy of that proverbial eagle's eye.

Vel, Sanjaya, Surasa, all names from Hindu mythology signalled the shift that the Lioness had brought to her country. From far left of Jyoti Basu & EMS Namboothiripad, to left of centre approach of Nehru, Indira and the other Gandhis, to finally far right of the Lioness. She was the greatest critic of Nehru's China policy, which culminated in the 1962 debacle, and the shame the country had to go through at the Chinese hands. Though some historians say it was the Indian aggressiveness that prompted the Chinese to attack and teach a lesson to India. The way they went back after having taken possession of up to Assam gives credence to this theory. Nehru and the then defence minister Krishna Menon's *Hindi-Chini Bhai Bhai* policy became a historic blunder that made the country a laughing stock after having to go through a war soon after. The Lioness had gone on record many times criticising Nehru for this fallacy that cost the country its morale.

But it was as if the Ghost of Nehru gave her a tight slap from his grave, as history repeated in Andamans. Like Nehru then, she was slowly but surely becoming a ridicule for the nation.

Chapter 40

The first of the *'Vel'* missiles that were synchronised with the *'Sanjaya'* satellite took flight in the late night hours, the night the whole of India was celebrating and therefore was awake for *'Shivratri'*. The auspicious night wherein the whole country revels in the glory of the destroyer, *Vel* missile exploded on the aircraft carrier, which was the backbone of Fa Hien. But the 75000 tonnes vessel was not an easy one to buckle. Reminiscent of King Kong versus Dara Singh, King Kong was capable of taking the hit. The aircraft carrier stood up against the assault, though heavily damaged in the process. Sinking it seemed to be a long shot for the missile.

Commander Latif but was not a naïve in the game. He knew the enormity of the aircraft carrier. The Stingray (Stingray-1, as it was coded) submarine was on its way for its first real life test. At thirty nautical miles speed, it had turned around the last of the cliffs. Now it was susceptible to be detected by the enemy vessels and submarines. Latif had not left this work to any of his colleagues since he knew that he had the chance to fire only one torpedo. That too needs to be fired at a vicinity and angle so that it could not get intercepted by enemy combats. He knew it was a suicidal mission.

Getting so close to a modern fleet will be a point of no return. He felt like Abhimanyu of *Mahabharat*, who was famously trapped inside the Chakravyuha (a circular army formation), who knew only to enter it but not to come out.

But the greater purpose of duty made him altruistic, and like Abhimanyu he also didn't feel the need to come out. Duty comes first.

By that time, Stingray-1 was dangerously close to the aircraft carrier, well within the striking range of even the enemy submarines and ships. Like the aircraft Enola Gay which infamously dropped 'Little Boy' over Hiroshima, the return path was fixed for Stingray-1. It's ironical that the pilot of Boeing B-29 named the aircraft after his mother Enola Gay and dropped a bomb nicknamed as Little Boy on a hapless population killing millions and is still considered a hero. That pilot had to turn a predetermined path to avoid the glares and clouds of the burst.

Herein Latif had to take a predetermined return path to save himself from a sure shot retaliatory strike. He therefore put the torpedo on the launch switch, took a last minute stock of the situation, and fired. Without waiting for any signals, he turned the submarine around and was on full throttle to a predetermined spot towards Bay of Bengal. Stingray-1 was on its fastest retreat, running for its survival. After a few moments, once things were stable and Latif felt that he was out of danger, he took stock of what happened and it almost froze him in incredulity. Stingray, which was capable of detecting any disturbance, was not giving any alarms. Suspiciously, he checked the status of the fired Torpedo. The status read:

"Launch aborted – Technical error".

Chapter 41

It didn't take the Chinese much time to figure out what had happened. Their accurate satellite monitoring systems gave the minutest details of from where the missile came. And in no time a dozen of Sukhoi-35 stealth bombers had surrounded the Barren Island. Within this time, another two missiles had already struck the aircraft carrier and this time the carrier was on its way down to the sea bed.

A Sukhoi-35 was equipped with the latest and most accurate ammunition. The air to surface missiles that fired in abundance made a mincemeat of the Indian camp. Thirty minutes later, when the bombers returned, there was no hope of even a rat coming out alive from the Indian hideout.

Far in the Indian mainland, the loss of lives and ammunition was definitely worrisome. But what struck them like a tsunami was the fact that Stingray failed to deliver. This was despite the numerous test drills carried out by the submarines on fake targets. In all those drills Stingrays fired in style. So, what failed them when it mattered the most?

Investigations were ordered to find out the loophole. The subs were taken back from service temporarily. The Russians were frantically called for. All hell broke loose in the higher echelons of power, but the news was kept a closely guarded secret, so that the opposition did not make hay while the sun shines.

The Russians, as usual, put the blame on Indian stubbornness to make the subs in India. They cited numerous cases worldwide wherein these submarines have worked with perfection. They even revealed some of the Russian undercover operations to prove their point, risking confidentiality.

Without wasting time, all the submarines sailed to Russia by the Russians to be thoroughly checked by them. Apart from a handful of key people not even a single soul was aware of this development. Russians wanted to check this not only in Indian interest, but for their interest as well. No, it was not the business interest of losing credibility with Indians. But to ascertain whether it was only the Indian ones that were affected or even their makes were also affected.

After a month's threadbare probe, Russians were both relieved as well as disturbed. Relieved because their makes were safe. Disturbed because, their friend India was very badly bugged by an enemy, and they were not in a position to pin-point that enemy.

The issue being so serious, the Russians sent back all the submarines with a clean chit. But the news was conveyed at a very high level, yes, to the Lioness, since they trusted nobody else.

Chapter 42

The next set of Stingrays, this time ten of them, were tendered by the Government and the competition was very intense. Unlike the earlier one, which was a cake walk for Waveproof, this time the state-run docks were equipped with Halocline simulations. A private manufacturer, notorious for its manipulating ability and to pull strings in the corridors of power, was also into the fray. Waveproof had to rely on its spotless execution track record.

The order estimated at Rs 60000 crores, was by any standards too big to chew for Waveproof. But the name it commanded in market by this time, propelled Ram to go for a quick debenture issue in the market. The debentures were taken like proverbial hot cakes by the investors. Soon Ram was flooded with funds of over than Rs 10000 crores as working capital and for Earnest Money Deposit.

The government was very accommodative allowing prorata payments and a staggered delivery schedule, thereby allowing smaller players like Waveproof to go for such big defence orders. Everything was set for Waveproof for the next paradigm shift, which would propel them to the league of bigger companies in India. It was prepared to get out of the mid-sized company league, which was always a hindrance when considered for big ticket orders.

But everyone got surprised when the Government finally decided to split the spoils. Waveproof was the highest bidder and the State run dock came out as the lowest. Government split the ten orders in the proportion of

5:3:2 among the lowest, second highest and highest bidders respectively. Normally, the industry norm was to split the spoils between the lowest two bidders. If a state-owned bidder is involved, then they become by default the second lowest bidder irrespective of what price they quoted. But even they have to match the price of the lowest bidder and take the allotted order. But herein the government's resolve to accommodate Waveproof, despite they being highest, was evident.

Rs 12000 crores order was not a small deal for Waveproof. Finally, it broke the glass ceiling to enter the league of heavy weights. But the euphoria was not visible to the extent it was expected to, since two submarines were too small for an order when compared to the expertise it had developed through the first set of orders.

But Ram was the only person happy with the development though he did not let it on his face. A sudden jump of Rs 12000 Crores is itself difficult to manage, what if the jump had been of Rs 30000 Crores. He had always believed that the growth should be palatable. Otherwise it could even finish off the company.

Chapter 43

Soon, the most ambitious manufacturing programme in India's defence history started off with much fanfare. The government received a lot of pats on its back, since they could rope in more players to the programme. The state-run dockyard as well as the large private sector player were addons to the programme as only Waveproof was trained for the job as part of the earlier trial order.

Government's decision to split the order over three parties was deliberate, so that, this time over they could make the life tougher for the forces who were there to sabotage the performance of the submarines. Moreover, they wanted one order to necessarily go to Waveproof as they wanted to look for what went wrong last time.

They were puzzled as they had anticipated such things well in advance and had picked up the possible loopholes to plug them in time. One such thing was KK. His escapades with the Russian blonde were well orchestrated by the government, to keep the idiot under control and therefore to prevent him from falling prey to enemy plans. This was supposedly a masterstroke played by the Indo-Russian intelligence network to prevent gullible guys from falling into the hands of other spy networks. The guys may think they were spilling the beans to enemies but were actually feeding information to their own government. This was a test for the loyalty of people as the ones who do not report this trap were best avoided for future assignments.

KK could never make out that the car accident and the subsequent captivation were all orchestrated by the Indian Intelligence. Thereafter, the “Double eye”, as they were called as apparently a version of the abbreviation for Indian Intelligence, kept KK well under the wraps. Such operations were carried out by Double Eye (2i) after an extensive profile mapping of key people. KK’s profile mapping convinced them that he was a potential loophole and had to be necessarily kept in check.

So, it was shocking for 2i, when they first heard of Latif’s INS Chamunda failing to deliver when it mattered the most. It was hard for them to believe that someone had outsmarted them. Dayanand Mudgal, who headed the 2i would have normally threw out many in his team for this intelligence failure. But people in the government’s close quarters were surprised to see no heads rolling.

Mudgal was very clear when it came to such hiccups. A knee-jerk reaction rather did more damage than the original setback. He was pretty confident about his team. If somebody has outsmarted him, he knew there could be a sabotage or back-stabbing somewhere. Disturbing the existing team would create a great number of ripples which will be a perfect camouflage for the culprit to get away. Mudgal was in fact answerable only to the Lioness, so he didn’t care a damn about what others thought.

It was his brain child that the government decided to include Waveproof also among the three winners of the bid. This he thought was necessary to catch the culprit red-handed. Knowing that intrusions have happened last time, it was clear that this time also the enemy will try to intrude with the new vendors. Hence, he did a ring fencing with intelligence officers all across the new vendors to prevent this. This exercise was done even before the bidding opened, since he knew all the three bidders were going to execute the projects on a piecemeal basis. The state-dockyard was filled up with 2i agents through government to government transfers. It was told that not even a fly could enter the dockyard or its office without a threadbare analysis of its history.

As far as the other private bidder was concerned, the founder-owner of it being very close to Lioness it was an easy game for Mudgal. Literally all the office premises, the dockyard, the cars of executives, their phones, their houses, even their drivers were bugged. Whatever happened in this company was getting tapped by 2i on an immediate basis.

Mudgal was not a novice to expect that the enemy will drive into his trap. Hence, he also kept an eye on the subvendors of these bidders. There were many foreign suppliers who supplied components and services to them. It was impossible to track all of them. Hence a technical agency under the garb of the third-party inspectors was injected into the project execution process, as a tender requirement. This agency was a government quality agency, which was by now studded with 2i agents.

But Mudgal was in a double mind on whether pursuing Waveproof would fetch him any results. Enemy would not be a fool to tread the beaten down path. He would not take risk since they knew that Waveproof's trial project would be under tight scrutiny now. But Mudgal had a gut feeling that Waveproof was where he should put his money on.

Chapter 44

Soon, the scene was set for the biggest rollout of domestic manufacturing in the Indian defence sector. Waveproof was present in that glittering function and the party was thrown open by the ministry in Delhi's Hyderabad House. Namy and Ram represented Waveproof, a rare occasion where both of them participated together. Otherwise it was either the Chairperson or the CEO who would participate in the functions. Ram had a point in pulling Namy into the function. The function was attended by the "who's who" of the defence industry. Having completed the trial order in style (its failure while in operation was a closely guarded secret), Waveproof was a prime candidate for winning orders from international clients even if on a contract manufacturing basis. Ram wanted the chairperson's presence to build relations and hence the business.

Ram's eyes were set on striking a deal any of the global biggies in the submarine industry who incidentally were all present there. Navantia from Spain, DCNS from Spain, ThyssenKrupp from Germany and many more. The function's real attraction though was the Lioness in her typical style. Lioness's gold embroidered saree shone like a sunny day amidst the rainy season. Her golden watch, high heeled sandals, ruby necklace and the umbrella shaped ear rings literally reminded the audience that age was just a number. It was natural that all the ladies there sulked with envy as the males could not shift their eyes from the Indian premier.

The three parties were called upon the stage for signing the contracts and were asked to address the gathering. The state-run Dockyard's claims to fulfil the commitments in time were greeted with the usual sarcasm, due to their long list of unfulfilled commitments. The large private player was also greeted with indifference since they were considered a manipulator and not expected to be serious in the long run. When Namy Ferrao rose for the talk, there was a deafening applause. It was testimony for the values she had stood for and the confidence she emanated amongst her peers. The question was who was more respected in the field, she or her company and many vouched for the former. The applause was so loud and clear that for a moment a glimpse of envy was clearly visible on the Lioness's face. Lioness never could stand the sight of someone else stealing the limelight. Those who noticed Lioness's annoyance dismissed it as a normal catfight. But those who knew her closely knew it as arrogance on her part which they all have experienced at one point or other.

Namy spoke about the wide vision her company held for India, especially its defence self-reliability. She highlighted the sacrifices the company had to make to fulfil the trial commitments and rise to her government's expectations. Clad in a light blue Bengal cotton saree, she was eloquent when it came to the commitment her team members had for this project. She had a special word of praise for Ram and his leadership that had turned around her company's fortunes. She stressed upon how they had to forego some commercial orders and put some others on the backburner in order to execute the defence trial project in time. She culminated the speech expressing her company's commitment towards India's development and the well-being of its people. One could see the child-like displeasure in the eyes of the other two company representatives when the crowd stood up to give Namy another round of applause. Green with envy was the right phrase to describe.

Chapter 45

Ram was literally surprised when the minister called upon him the next day and wanted KK to continue as the SBU-Head for submarines. He was not expecting such kind of interference from the ministry. But all that he had heard from the media about the Lioness was turning out to be true. Ram had, in fact, by this time made up his mind to put Shikhar at the top job, since after the trials he was not getting the right vibes from the ministry. His sixth sense was always smelling a rat somewhere.

Since he had to somehow keep the ministry in good humour, KK was allowed to continue, but in fact Ram did some ruthless plans as well. Soon though, another command came from the ministry. They conveyed their decision to station Commander Latif as a special duty officer. And they wanted Latif to be provided an office each in the Head Quarters as well as the dockyard. As special duty officer he should have access to anything and everything in the project. This was discomforting Ram and he questioned the ministry's intentions. But the answer was a cold stare from the visiting ministry official followed by the appointed order initialled by the Defence minister. Knowing that the defence minister is nothing but a puppet of Lioness, he knew the futility of showing further resistance. In his mind he cursed the plain dictatorship in the country and on the fact that democracy had become a joke.

Commander Latif walked in with grace to the Waveproof office to a hero's welcome. Though lackadaisical in heart, Ram welcomed him with a warm smile. KK was on his side while Latif plainly told Ram that "whether you like it or not, I'm to enter and exit your office premises as per my wish. Next time onwards no one should care about me coming or doing anything here, lest it bothers me. Hope you understand that we military guys do not enjoy civilian company much." He patted on the shoulder of a stunned Ram, and asked him to take it easy. "This is the military way of straight talk, please do not take it to heart Mr Ram. You are my good friend, and will remain so," were his words of comfort.

It did not take much time for Latif to be part of Waveproof routine. But his timings in the office were always unpredictable. Deliberately so. After his initial few months in office, Latif started developing his own coterie. He had this knack of getting closer to people whom he thought will be useful. And Bala was one of those chosen ones. Bringing Bala to the Headquarters team was the handiwork of Ram, since eventually he wanted to throw out KK and bring in Shikhar as SBU-Head. Bala but by this time had become very close to the partying circuits of KK's coterie, aka Hyderabad-gang. Shikhar but was very much keen to have Bala with him and had recommended his name to Ram in one of their closed door meetings.

Bala being in charge for all the Quality inspections, had a grip over who all visits the dockyard for this project. It was this information that Latif was aiming at. Soon Bala became a frequent visitor to Mumbai Naval club with Latif. Mumbai club had the elegance of its own. Bala was seeing such an ambience for the first time. He could not believe that he is in midst of an otherwise chaotic Mumbai. The air and elegance of a military space was something the civilians always got amused about.

It was one of those evenings that Latif had taken Bala out. Bala was all praise for Latif as he had that gift of the gab to keep listeners intact. They as usual settled for that corner table which gave a clear view of the famed Queen's necklace in Mumbai. Sun had set already but the dusky light rays were still hovering around like abandoned pets. Latif ordered for his favourite Absolut Vodka and the waiter knowingly made it a Martini, shaken not stirred. Latif was a die-hard fan of Sean Connery's James Bond, and while in the club always drank the drink James Bond was fond of. Bala looked around for his brand of Cognac and ordered it with ice and Thums up. Latif asked the waiter to pause, gave a small lecture on the origins of brandy to Bala and asked him to drink with Soda and not Thums up. He also asked him to skip the ice cubes and drink it in a slightly warm glass. The aroma of Cognac aka Brandy is best at room temperature or slightly warmer than that. The Connoisseurs prefer warming up the glass with their hands before pouring Cognac to enjoy the aroma. Bala was enjoying these tips from the sophisticated world of drinking.

They were through with their first rounds and ordered for a second along with some fried Bombay duck and Masala Tiger prawns. The first round should be finished without any snacks was the advice Latif had for his novice colleague. But with the second round progressing, two more people joined them uninvited. They spoke to Latif as if they knew each other since ages. The camaraderie was clearly visible. But Bala was not amused with them just barging in without introduction, more so because Latif also did not care to introduce Bala to them.

As if having read Bala's mind, Latif glanced at him and smiled. "Bala, these people are from the Government of India and you need to know them as Mr. Shakespeare and Mr. Shelly only. Both of them want to know certain things about the trial submarine orders executed at your place. You can find them in the import freight forwarding agency office as employees. That way they can be in regular touch with you", Latif laid out his long drawn plans for Bala. Though dumbstruck, Bala nodded in submission.

Latif wanted Bala to visit the freight forwarder's office every Wednesday and Friday for updates. Shakespeare and Shelly, though irregular with the attendance, soaked up all the details from Bala, of not only the trial order but also what was happening in the current order. And it was during one of those chat sessions that Bala spoke about a new software that was introduced in the submarines, though the Russians were not very keen on that. The software, which was developed by a Finnish company was to keep a fleet of Stingrays automatically synchronised, so that they were in reach of each other to help and strategize the attacks. It was like a shepherd keeping the flock together. And rightfully the software was named 'Camaraderie'.

Chapter 46

There was a rat race between the three companies to roll out the first submarine. Waveproof obviously had a head start due to their trial order experience, but the large private player was fast catching up, true to their image of a champion in execution. Ram was totally focussed on making this job a prestige issue and wanted to pip all the competitors. He knew that a successful execution would fetch him a bonanza of manufacturing orders from foreign companies. In his zest to succeed, however, he became totally oblivious of the thread bare intelligence activities going on in his company. Though the name was 2i, effectively they had a million eyes open on whatever happened in Waveproof.

Ram's pet project of commercial ships which actually turned around the company was starting to feel the heat due to this hype and hoopla on defence projects. The hype was making his current as well as potential foreign shipping customers jittery of losing priority at Waveproof. Ram had read into their minds and wanted to set the things right before the damage was done. That was when he raked up this in the all-important board meeting.

He started off with the popular phrase 'One in hand is worth two in the bush'. He cautioned the group about the euphoria on defence projects getting too much into their heads. He said defence projects were more like a wavering carrot in front of the donkey. Companies were at the mercy of precarious government policies, erratic and high-headed technology providers from across the seas and a hostile international community who builds opinion against weapon manufacturers and thereby try to isolate them. He was of the opinion that his company cannot build its future only on defence jobs. Waveproof should continue to showcase to the world that it always was committed to commercial ships and would continue to do so.

And Ram had a clear game plan as to how he should assuage the hurt sentiments of customers. He said as a major shift he would transfer KK as the new boss of commercial ships from his present position as head-Defence SBU. This would send the right signals to the market as the champion of defence manufacturing is being shifted to commercial segment to give a boost to that business. The Board was aghast at the sudden change being proposed. But more were to come. He said Shikhar is being proposed as the new Defence-head. Since Ram had already discussed everything with Namy prior to the meeting and obtained her nod, he was at his confident best.

"The defence trial orders and the foray into mainstream defence manufacturing was only a publicity stunt to prove a point to the world of our prowess. I was sure that the hype would certainly increase our name recall in customer minds. Also, defence manufacturing being more stringent as far as quality was concerned, the commercial segment would treat us with more respect, increasing our price realisation. In short, it is this price premium and nothing else that I wanted from our foray into defence space. Now that we have achieved what we want, I want the focus to shift to our bread and butter business. It's time that we come back to reality." – Ram quoted the famous management guru Al Ries and concluded by saying, "The basic approach of positioning is not to create something new and different, but to manipulate what's already up there in the mind, to retie the connections that already exist."

The board was silent for some time and finally when it sunk down, started clapping at the genius of Ram. Ram had a stoic smile on his face as he knew nobody knew the actual reason why he shunted KK out of defence business. Apart from his sixth sense that made him feel something wrong was going on, he also wanted to send a message to the ministry not to meddle in his business. In Waveproof, there was only one boss, and the message was clear.

Chapter 47

Ram's announcement to the outside world about the changes coincided with another big-ticket news, one which he held up his sleeves. It was a big order for commercial ships from a Swedish shipping company, which was of Rs 6500 crores, to be executed over a period of six years. The news about the order gave the subtle message to the ministry that Waveproof did not care a hoot about what they thought about KK's exit from the defence business.

Internally Shikhar's elevation caused a lot of heart burns in the close circles KK had created. They were worried about Shikhar coming down heavily on whoever was close to KK. But Shikhar in his inaugural address in the division, assuaged all such fears and said he would bring no changes at all for the first year at the helm of affairs.

Shikhar's foremost challenge in the job was to come out of the image of being a proxy of Ram. Though it was difficult, he had to prove a point and come out of the shadows of Ram. And what better opportunity than when Ram had shifted focus elsewhere. Shikhar was convinced that it was now or never.

And soon, he got the opportunity he had been waiting for. The Russian Stingrays that were operating near the black sea off the coast of Kharkhiv were always wary of the western support to Ukraine. The submarines were always on the lookout for the western forces trying to build up forces along the Ukrainian coast. But what the Russians were not aware was the high technology spy satellites installed by the west under the garb of blue chip technology companies. Russian intelligence was regularly reporting highly frequent western contacts over the black sea, but submarines were never able to detect any suspicious ship movements. Russians after some time could smell something was wrong with their surveillance. Their reach in the western intelligence network pointed them towards the inability of stingrays to camouflage themselves from the high frequency sonic wave scanning. The sonic wave transmitters placed on the sea bed effectively sent the sonic waves across the sea. These waves were captured by floating receptors on the sea surface and were converted into electro-magnetic waves and transmitted into space. The spy satellites took inference from the pattern of these waves and spotted the under-sea movements of the submarines. So, it became a child's play for the western ships to dodge and sometimes misguide these submarines.

It was at this juncture that the Russians shared their dilemma with their good friends, the Indians. Unless this drawback was addressed, they were sure it would affect the future defence sales with India. Even otherwise, the Lioness had to take criticism from the opposition on the inferior technology of the Russians that could put the country in trouble when pitted against the enemies wielding new age technologies from the west. Russians were particularly looking at the Indian expertise and acumen in soft technologies, which could not only salvage their business with Indians but also bring their products at par with the west.

Bangalore-based Indian Institute of Science (IISc) was the premier research institution in India. Moreover, it was

Shikhar's alma mater. So, when the question came about plugging the lapse in Stingrays, he decided to approach his alma mater.

Chapter 48

Shikhar's intention after taking over the Defence SBU was clear. He wanted to execute these orders before the other two companies could. If he disturbed the apple cart only to settle personal scores, he knew he could falter on execution. He thought the best way to score one-up against KK was to beat his track record in execution.

Shikhar's only pain in the arse was the presence of the defence personnel in his office. It was as if two handsome guys never want to be together. Though Shikhar was far more aged than Latif, his looks were more elegant than the younger guy. The younger guy though scored over with his impeccable mannerisms. A military man stands out with his mannerisms, and Shikhar hated somebody outsmarting his charms. But his only solace was the erratic presence of Latif in the office.

The news of 'Camaraderie' software created a flutter in defence ministry. They were totally unaware of such a software. The immediate reaction of the ministry was to seal the activities in Waveproof and take all suspects there to interrogation. But better sense prevailed when Dayanand Mudgal took the Lioness in confidence and stalled that preposterous move.

Naturally the fingers pointed towards KK though Mudgal as chief of 2i, was pretty sure that KK was incapable of doing such things. But for the sake of it, KK was ordered to be picked up. The challenge was how to pull him in without raising suspicions.

It was at this point that Latif pointed out to Mudgal that KK was right then without holding any portfolio, since he was yet to be formally appointed as the head of commercial ships, a position Ram could not give away so easily. For name-sake he was given the post of project advisor to the CEO.

Soon the ministry raked up a committee called Defence Advisory Council. Along with the usual names from FICCI and CII, KK's name was proposed by the Defence Minister. And since that would keep KK away from Mumbai, Ram fully endorsed that.

KK's interrogation was done by Shakespeare and Shelly, nicknames of agents Pritam and Manpreet respectively. Pritam and Manpreet, having had enough exposure already to Waveproof, thanks to Bala, made KK parrot the events during execution verbatim. KK, due to fear, admitted that he was being used by an unknown set of people and was coerced into a honey trap. He explained one by one what all information he had divulged to his oppressors. Once he was about to complete his submissions, two people walked in asking KK, "You never told us about Camaraderie!" KK was flabbergasted to see them and suddenly sulked with fear. "Don't worry man, you were divulging the details to your own country men, nothing to worry. But somebody it seems has outsmarted all of us. We need your help to catch the traitor in the boat, oops, submarine." KK could not believe his eyes that the guys he thought as his tormentors were actually Indian agents.

With Pritam and Manpreet adding what they had learnt, the two 'tormentors', who identified as agents Saurav and Kurian started joining the dots. The software was sold during the final commissioning stages of first trial submarine. After checking the sale value, jaws dropped at 2i Head Quarters. A proprietary software of this stature would have cost at least 2 million US dollars in the international market. The value stated by Waveproof stood at a paltry Rs 45 Lakhs. A similar software that was bought by the air force to keep its herd of F16s together costed a whopping 6 million US dollars, that being a proprietary add-on software of Lockheed Martin.

Within a week the whole communication regarding this software in the Waveproof computers were copied down by Bala and given to Latif. There was nothing in those emails and invoices which were utterly conspicuous. The software was supplied by a dealer in Dubai. It was just because of curiosity that Latif pressed Ctrl+F and searched the Dubai dealer's name Al Kareema Agencies.

Supposedly an automobile spares dealer, it was giving software services to Waveproof. Something was amiss, Latif was sure.

Chapter 49

Bur Dubai was once the most sought-after area in Dubai, till the new upmarket ones like Jumeirah took over. But like Nariman Point in Mumbai, it still commands an old-world charm. The Bank Street in Bur Dubai still had the best names in the banking industry though their main Dubai branches had shifted elsewhere, in search of better business concentrations. Latif, after having taken an Air India flight to Sharjah purposefully, had taken a taxi to reach the Bur Dubai office of Al Kareema Agencies LLC. He had taken help from the Dubai police through Interpol. After the extradition treaty signed between India and UAE in 1998 at the initiative of the then Indian home minister, Mr. L.K. Advani, the Dubai police could not have said no to the Indian request. Not because it came through the Interpol, but because of the growing importance of India in the region. With USA's receding interest in the region, smaller and vulnerable countries were looking forward to a new saviour for them. Especially the kingdoms that always carried the insecurity of being dethroned by popular democracy movements. Also, the infighting between the Arabian kingdoms added to their insecurity. It was then that the Indian government signed a security pact with the kingdom to secure them as if it was an Indian territory. Indian sincerity was evident when they took all the risk to take on the might of China in Doklam to secure Bhutanese territory. After that, literally the smaller nations queued up to get an endorsement from India, who was less intimidating when compared to its peers like USA and China. The Lioness became the darling in the region not for her looks but for her guts.

It was a Sunday morning, and the bank street offices were coming alive after the extended weekend which included the holiday on Thursday on account of the death of the king of Abu Dhabi who was instrumental in the construction of the Burj Khalifa. Dubai was then relenting from a debt trap further aggravated by a real estate slump. Half-way through, ambitious and prestigious project of world's tallest building, was almost wound up due to the sinking economy. It was then that the oil rich Abu Dhabi came to the rescue and gave a helping hand. As a matter of gratitude, the building was named Burj Khalifa, after the king of Abu Dhabi. The originally envisaged name was Burj Dubai, i.e., the Fort of Dubai. The tall structure which was visible from Bur Dubai pointed far into the sky, as if philosophically telling the onlookers to look towards the heaven for solutions.

The sudden roar of a Ferrari engine shook Latif from his thoughts. He was dressed as a perfect banker and walked into the office of Mashreq Bank. An officer from the Indian consulate in Dubai was waiting for him there. Sridevi, as she introduced herself, was an IFS officer in her probation, as per records. But the IPS officer who was a couple of years into her career with the Indian intelligence 2i, had well masqueraded her role as a pivotal intelligence officer on duty. The six feet stout woman had a stunning personality and if not for the conservative middle-east crowd anybody would have taken her for a cop. They settled in one of the couches provided by the bank for its privileged customers. Indian consulate did have an account there. The Bank which had its internal furnishings done in a typical Jordanian fashion, had long chandeliers with gold plated frames. The green light gelled well with the turquoise green walls and the Pista green curtains. With all greenery around, Sridevi broke the ice poking Latif, "Are you green with envy with our Arabian lifestyle, officer?" She chuckled.

Latif shrugged off the comment with a customary grin and sat closer to the girl to give a feeling to the onlookers that they were a couple. The girl blushed with an accepting smile. She seemed to be enjoying the company of a handsome man.

After hearing what Sridevi told him, Latif could not hide his surprise and despite his best efforts to hide his emotions, started smiling at the revelation. From the preliminary information he had gathered while in India, he was wondering what an automobile spares trader could do in software. Now after hearing out from Sridevi he had no more qualms.

In five minutes, both of them had walked into Al Kareema office on the adjoining street with the pomp and gaiety of Mashreq Bank officials.

Chapter 50

The Al Kareema office bore the look of an Indian salon.If Indian salons, especially in Mumbai, carried the posters of Amitabh Bachchan, Rajesh Khanna and the Khans off late, this Dubai office carried the posters of Mercedes convertible, Ferrari GP and Cadillacs. A Filipino sat at the front desk as expected. Filipinos had off late dominated the job markets in the middle-east because of their English-speaking ability and enterprising spirit.

Seeing the Indians, Balvinder Sandhu welcomed the two visitors to his cabin in Hindi. It was amusing to see that like in India, even in the middle-east, the automobile spares sector was dominated by the Sikhs. In typical Sardarji style, he ordered for two glasses of *Mango Lassi* for the guests. After the niceties, the conversation was mainly on the financing requirements for the business. As expected, he started cribbing on the fall of crude oil prices and the adverse effect on Gulf-economies because of that. The sale of new cars had gone down drastically and people had curbed spending on maintenance also. Across the board, recession in the economy was being felt. He blamed it on Saudi Arabia and USA playing a "who will blink-first game." It was when they offered a loan for his Indian business, that his face suddenly lightened up. They offered a loan in India without any collaterals. Sandhu was delighted.

As a legal formality of the loan, Sandhu had to share all the ownership details of his business. As he was sharing the details Latif winked at Sridevi, who put her spy camera on.

On their way back, they stepped into Mashreq Bank and thanked the branch manager for the help. The loan was surely not to be sanctioned, the bank would find a reason not to process the loan.

Balvinder Sandhu was a happy man that day, and he decided to leave home a bit early. He thought he could take his wife and two daughters for an outing. The falling crude oil prices had made him think twice whether to continue forever in the gulf region. He was thinking of shifting base back to India for two reasons. His parents were old and it was getting difficult for them to manage themselves. Secondly India's growth story was like a fairy tale and the international community was gung-ho about Indian prospects. Naturally as an Indian he was feeling that he would miss the bus if he did not migrate back now.

So, when this offer of a huge loan at an interest rate at par with stable international rates came, he thought this is the right opportunity to spill the beans with his family.

When he broke the news of his serious intentions to move back to India, his daughters went berserk. Who would want to leave the cosiness of one of the world's best cities to the lurch of an over-populated nation where life meant struggle? Understandably so, his daughters' adverse and violent reaction was expected. Sandhu looked at his wife for help. Even she was not in favour of moving back to India. She knew the plight of a Punjabi daughter–in-law destined to look after her in laws. Hence, she moved away her face, showing her discontentment.

Sandhu was in a married man's dilemma wherein to heed to whose wishes, mother's or wife's or daughter's. Finally, he did what all married men do; he got into his car and showed his frustration on the pedal. Apparently frightened at the break-neck speed and the kind of shrieking halt he made once reaching the car porch at home, the family said yes to his plans of moving back.

But Balvinder Sandhu was to get extradited to India as per the extradition treaty signed between India and UAE, which he did not know then.

Chapter 51

Shikhar Khetrapal received a standing ovation in the Annual General Body meeting where he was a special invitee. The ministry had sent him in particular and Waveproof in general a citation. He was lauded for the extraordinary pace with which the work of the first Stingray submarine had been carried out, much ahead of the two other manufacturers. Though both Ram and Namy were quite surprised at the Ministry's seemingly hasty recognition since there was one more submarine to be manufactured as part of the contract, they did not want to kill the euphoria and morale.

Shikhar replaced KK in the ministry's Council of Experts, thus exacting a silent revenge. And very soon the ministry called for a meeting of council members with the defence minister. Shikhar was enjoying the new status to the hilt especially when the minister had a very special word of praise for his company. Minister was very impressed with the fact that a comparatively smaller company has managed to outsmart its larger counterparts both in taking orders and executing them well.

So, when he was asked by the staff to stay back after the meeting, Shikhar was expecting more accolades from the minister. But despite waiting for more than a couple of hours there were no signs of minister calling him in. When the wait became longer he started becoming restless. To his surprise none of the staff members who had asked him to stay back, were present there.

His wait came to an end when Shakespeare and Shelly patted him on the back. Shikhar was having a glass of water from the water cooler, and he hated somebody touching his body informally. He cocked his head to show his displeasure but turned back meekly after seeing the two well-built guys standing in an intimidating manner.

"Minister is in the Hyderabad house, we came to take you there", Shakespeare told him while holding Shikhar's hand and gesturing to move. When Shikhar showed resistance, Shelley pushed him from behind saying, "*chal, saale* (Move you spoiled brat)". Shikhar got the message and he tried to escape. Shakespeare and Shelley, true to their name had to invent some new names for Shikhar and had to culminate it with a tight slap over his face. Shikhar's looks clearly said it was all over, for him.

The white Ambassador car that was waiting in the porch sped off the moment Shikhar was pushed to the back seat and both his tormentors sandwiched him. Shikhar felt as if inside a stampede when both the heavyweights purposefully jammed him, each time the car took a twist or turn. Delhi's sweltering heat, maddening traffic and this manhandling had drained him off by the time they reached an old dilapidated building. The building was of the British era, with red bricks showing its bleeding face here and there where the plasters had torn off. The policeman on security did his customary salute and went back to his umbrage under the Peepul tree. It was then that he read the obscure name board on the building.

The Indian Intelligence had the eagle eye as its emblem surrounded by a ring with 'Indian Intelligence' written on it. The car dropped them off in the portico and moved out into the sun again. Seeing Shikhar reluctant to step inside, Shakespeare mocked him, "Step in with your right leg sir. Bring in some luck for us." The sweet talk of Shakespeare was set off by the grumping of Shelley from behind when he screamed, "*Aage chal behenchod* (Move over, you sister-fucker)."

'Dayanand Mudgal-Director' The name plate outside the cabin door gave the impression of a school principal's office. Deserted as if no one wanted to go near it, the corridor had a lonely sofa placed for waiting people. The sofa did not have the sophistication of a director's office and it shrieked like a piles patient when the three of them put their heavy asses on it. And like all the typical government offices an old fan rotated in a very slow speed as if to show the onlookers this is what happens to everyone during old age.

A double bell rang and a peon in uniform rushed inside. After a moment, peon came outside and asked Shakespeare to take everyone upstairs and wait in the interrogation room. "Interrogation room?" exclaimed Shakespeare with a sympathetic look at Shikhar, winking at Shelley. Shelley also nodded in sympathy. Shikhar was about to piss in his pants.

Chapter 52

Shakespeare and Shelley were in for a pleasant surprise when it was Latif and not Mudgal who greeted them. "So, you finally had him, Pritam? Did he trouble you? Anyway, Manpreet accompanies you not without a reason." Latif was posing the question at Shakespeare whose real name was Pritam Pal Singh. Manpreet Sodhi alias Shelley beamed with pride after hearing a compliment for his physical prowess.

Latif then shifted his attention to a sulking Shikhar, who was wanting to flee like a caged parrot. Shikhar's dislike to see Latif moving around in Waveproof was known to everyone. "Now you know why I was moving around in your office? I was knowing from day one that you were the crooked one in the lot and not that loudmouth KK. And your abhorrence for me made my hunch stronger. I was fully aware of you bullying over Bala, trying to supervise what all he talked and shared with us. You simply did not know to what extent we had bugged your office".

"So, tell me about your brother-in-law's business in Dubai and your connections with him. It is not that we don't know about it, but we would like to hear it from the horse's mouth. Tell us how much money you earned for putting that bug software in the submarines. And most importantly on whose behalf you did it? Shikhar, you have done the gravest kind of crime, which is unpardonable. Had it been in strict middle-east countries, they would have beheaded you by now. Fortunately, you live in one of the greatest democracies in the world, which believes that not even one innocent should be punished even if a thousand culprits are exonerated. And you have tried to thwart the security of that country, which has its foundations built on *Ahimsa.* A country once the richest in the world but was systematically plundered over three centuries by the invaders, just because it never learned to protect itself. And finally, when it was standing on its own shoulders you wanted to undermine it. I can well finish off you creating a fake encounter, and nobody would even get a whiff of it. But wait, you can help us. Help us find out the real culprits who wanted you to do this. You were just a tool in somebody else's greater game plan. Guide us on that, I'll do something for you, Shikhar. People do mistakes, come on, and let us now think for our country".

Latif's long talk was observed with awe by both the cops, but with fear by Shikhar. The good cop bad cop strategy was being tried, and they were sure they would be asked to play the bad cop. What inspired them was that Latif was never getting pumped up and was cool as a cucumber. But all that impression changed when they saw his next move. Latif put on the laptop and turned the screen towards them. "If you don't want to heed to what I said, and would want to remain defiant, this is what awaits you." He switched on a video. The video had excerpts from a famous Hindi movie, *Saza-e-Kalapani*, which filmed the tortures in the Andaman jails by the British. The tortured were the Indian nationalists who raised their voice against the imperialistic atrocities. "It's now time to return the favours, to torture the people who try to scuttle this great nation. And when it comes to my nation, I show no mercy on the traitors. Is the message clear, you bastard?" The questions ended with a deafening slap on Shikhar's face.

Pritam and Manpreet had dropped their inhibitions of playing bad cops. Here was a split personality in front of them, and they felt they were no more needed. And they were seeing a military man in action for the first time. And like amateur sportsmen who would want to see professionals play, they just wanted to sit back and enjoy the officer-in-action.

Chapter 53

Shikhar's interrogation led the investigation towards his financial gains. Most of his gains were stashed in Dubai, being pumped in to his brother-in-law Balvinder Sandhu's business. But Sandhu was getting jittery day by day and wanted to get rid of this thorny crown from his head. That explained his wish to return to India on the pretext of looking after his parents. The explanation given by Shikhar for the source of income was that he was siphoning off the profits of the company, hand-in-gloves with other senior management. But Sandhu, an astute Punjabi, was wondering how come such things happen at Waveproof, which was highly profitable and had the reputation of being one of the well-run companies in the country. That had rung warning bells in his mind that Shikhar was hiding something.

Balvinder Sandhu's dilemma whether to succumb to his family's wish to stay back in Dubai or shift to India to avoid an ordeal soon came to an end. There was a team of Dubai police and Interpol who picked him up based on information from India. Sandhu was clueless when asked for his sudden spurt in income and had to take Shikhar's name of out of desperation. That filled the dots for the cops.

Latif though had failed to hear from Shikhar on whose behalf he was sabotaging the country. The interrogation team had started third degree methods to take out the information, but then Latif stopped them. Latif somehow had a hunch that Shikhar was just a conduit and he was not genuinely aware of finer details. It was obviously so because such international espionage cases work on multi-levels of secrecy.

Latif decided to explore further into Waveproof and for that it was required to hide what had happened to Shikhar. Soon, Waveproof received the circular citing the ministry's decision to indefinitely hold Shikhar back in Delhi for the formulation of an important national defence directive.

By now it was clear to National agencies that a clear case of espionage had happened in Waveproof compromising the efficiency and confidentiality of Stingrays. The strategic failure of Stingrays in Andaman was no longer a case of accident. It was the brain child of an enemy to dysfunction the strategic national weapons. Now the questions to be answered were, who was doing it, and how deep is the malice? Was it confined only to Stingrays or are spread out to other weapons also? It was disturbing question for everyone assembled in that small room in 2i headquarters. There was a worried look on Dayanand Mudgal's face, something his colleagues had never seen before. Slowly the worried face turned into a determined face. As if absent-minded, he slowly walked out of the room without acknowledging anybody and entered his cabin. The door was shut tightly behind him.

Chapter 54

The funds that came to Sandhu on behalf of Shikhar had their origins in Switzerland. And Switzerland being a haven of parked black money, it was impossible for the government to figure out the source. But Dayanand Mudgal was known for making impossible things possible. What he wanted to tap was India's talent in information technology, which was second to none.

Mudgal's flight arrived in the Kempegowda international airport at Bengaluru in the late hours. Bengaluru which was infamous for its traffic woes, comes alive though in style in the nights. Karnataka government had sent him a car with adequate security, and the car was without any government insignia on it so as not to invite any unwanted attention.

The chief of 2i was all praise for the Bengaluru Development Authority that had brought in novel ways to ease the traffic. They had made small fly overs and under passes to skip over the perennial bottlenecks. He had crossed the Windsor Manor underpass and was about to take the left turn towards Mount Carmel college to take that short cut towards Raj Bhavan.

Late hours in Bengaluru witnessed many accidents due to drunken driving. Bengaluru was a city of pubs and the climate throughout the year was cold and conducive for drinking.

Moreover, being a cash-rich city due to the money from the flourishing software industry, it was subjected to the maximum number of drunken driving accidents. The road adjacent to the golf course starting from Sankey road police station to Windsor Manor was infamous for such crashes because of the trees on road side and the undue curvature of the road.

A speeding Mahindra LCV coming towards Windsor Manor jumped the road divider and crashed into Mudgal's Toyota Innova. The truck hit the car on the rear and since the car was already turning left, instead of overturning the car, it actually pushed it further. Mudgal sprung forward from the seat due to the impact, but the seat belt prevented him from a fatal hit against the front seat. Mudgal's driver did not know what hit him, but did not lose presence of mind. Fortunately for them, the road was deserted at that late hour and the car speeding ahead did not hit any object. Fifty metres ahead there was a traffic island which came handy in stopping the car, as the car went and barged into it.

Within twenty minutes, the top brass of the Karnataka police had assembled there to escort the 2i chief into the safety of Raj Bhavan.

Chapter 55

Dr Shankaralingam was in a mediocre attire that day too.

His reluctance to wear a coat and suit despite being the director of Indian Institute of Science (IISc) was deep rooted in the hatred he had for the country's dependence on foreign technology. Seventy years of freedom and the nation was still dependent on foreign technology except for a handful of areas like space and information technology. His half sleeve khadi shirt and a black trouser was a hallmark identity not only across IISc but across the technology fraternity in the country.

Mudgal's resolve to meet Mr. Lingam on the next day itself was to give a clear signal to the perpetrators of the previous day's accident that, come what may, they cannot shake his mind. Lingam was in his humorous best when he imitated Mudgal's typical mannerism. Mudgal had this habit of leaning forward a bit too much while shaking hands. Lingam, having met him many times in the Prime Minister's office, had noted about this mannerism and was spontaneous to make fun of it this time. Both Lingam and Mudgal were, at a time, part of the Prime Minister's Advisory council.

After the niceties, Lingam heard Mudgal and delved into a deep thought. Bengaluru's famed filter coffee was getting cold next to his writing pad. A Bangalorean allowing his filter coffee to get cold was unheard off, unless his mind was totally distracted and disturbed. Mudgal's anxious silence and Lingam's deep thoughts were disturbed only by the grumbling ceiling fan. It kept on grumbling as like a child crying for attention.

"Have you heard about Julian Assange or Edward Snowden, Mr. Mudgal?" Lingam's sudden question woke him up from the half-slumber caused by the fabled Bengaluru weather. The question caught Mudgal by surprise and he was pondering what to answer. Obviously, he had heard about these two people, but that was not the intent of the question. As if reading his mind, "What Mudgal, you are the chief of our intelligence, if they can do such a stuff, why can't we also try the same?" Lingam paused for a moment and continued. "I can do this for you with the help of my brilliant boys, but we need anonymity and legal protection by the government, without any conditions by you."

Mudgal thought for a moment and nodded, "Professor, nothing can be more important for the nation than this; be rest assured that you have the full backing of the Prime Minister. All your conditions have been accepted. We do not have much time; this cancer must have spread to, God only knows which all defence projects. We need to find the rot before it scuttles the nation."

Lingam's face was basking in the glory that the nation was dependent on his institute and, therefore, on him. But this was not the first time his coveted institute had guarded the nation. Mudgal had this in mind when he told about the special jackets the institute had made for the soldiers who guard Siachen, and how cooperative the then director, Mr. Srikanth Mudholkar, was. He made it a point to poke Lingam by commenting how down to earth and unassuming Mr Mudholkar was and how he never asked any questions, leave alone putting any conditions. Lingam being astute, took the hint but gave it back on the same coin. He knew Mudgal and Mudholkar belong to the same region Raichur in Karnataka and in all probability should be known to each other, if not related to each other. He made an intelligent guess and commented, "Your affection for kindred people is understood, but I stick to my conditions Mr Mudgal. If you agree we go forward, otherwise no." Lingam was assertive when he said no.

Chapter 56

Indian prowess in the IT sector was never an overstatement. Mudgal was beaming with pride when he presented the findings to the PMO. Lingam and his team of ethical hackers had hacked into the Swiss bank industry servers. It was like child's play for these geniuses who were otherwise trained to withstand hacking challenges from unfriendly countries. The findings threw up some prominent names who were kingpins in the international espionage, arms deal and narcotics business. These three businesses were like off springs of the same species—always interconnected.

But what worried 2i was the fact that the names were all known names, the usual suspects. And it is common that these people were involved in such crimes as middlemen. These people were actually a camouflage used by the real culprits. But looking at the data, one thing had struck his mind. Money had flown to Swiss banks from a particular location near to Kensington in London. And this region was infamous for being a high-concentration area of banks, arms dealers, money launderers, international financial fraud fugitives, spies and prostitutes. Searching for the origin of this money was like looking for a particular Casino fraudster in Las Vegas.

London being the nerve centre of such nefarious activities, not only 2i, but most of the intelligence agencies had their strong presence there. Mudgal had put his agents on the job already. It was one of these agents who spotted a high payment being transferred to an Indo-French cultural group that matched the details Lingam had provided. This group's main activity was to promote Indian and French cultures at both places. They had a plethora of people who were experts in both French and various Indian languages.

This was the only opening Mudgal could find to explore. Within the next few days, the intelligence authorities scanned the whole lot of people who travelled in and out of India under the aegis of this group. Most of them were students from either side under an exchange program. This exchange program was a very popular one across India and was spread out into the rural areas also.

With such a sporadic spread, 2i was really perplexed how to get a clue from this. Then it suddenly struck them to explore the Russian angle. They were sure that the same agency must have been used to put a foothold in Russia, to make sure what transpired between Indians and Russians in Russia. And the best way was to check the existing Indo-French list with the Franco-Russian list. 2i with their excellent relations with the Russians found it easy to convince them to probe into this agency and their movements in Russia.

The long list provided by the Russians finally opened a window for 2i.

Chapter 57

There were four names that were common among the Indian and Russian lists. And it was highly unlikely that the French interpreters for India could act as interpreters for Russia as well. If four names were appearing common the reason had to be something more than mere interpretation and cultural exchange. Out of four, one name was easily eliminated as it was a person of Russian origin. She belonged to Siberia and was in France to study French Classical anthology.

Out of the rest, further elimination was not needed. Because, the time of one person's presence was too obvious to be a coincidence.

Tatiana Onopriienko was born to a French mother and a Ukrainian father. Her mother had to raise her alone since her father died in a nuclear disaster. He was one of those hapless fire-fighters deputed by the Soviet Union to douse the fire caused at Chernobyl in 1986. The poor fellows didn't know that they were being exposed to a radiation level of 6000 millisieverts (msv). The kind of secrecy maintained behind the iron curtain prevented the exact cause of death from being known to the kith and kin. It was told that he lost his life in a fire accident.

Once USSR broke in 1991, the western world tried to salvage the nuclear plants. In the process, they collected the information about the deceased, and that was when Tatiana who was a toddler first saw her mother seething with revenge on the Russians. Once having resettled in France thanks to her roots in

Toulouse, Taty was brought up with this hatred for the Russians. That but didn't prevent the little girl from learning Russian as a second language. She took it due to an affinity for her Father whose affection she missed throughout. Russian was the predominant language in parts of Ukraine bordering Belarus and Russia, and her father's mother tongue was Russian.

Her mother had refused to re-marry and continued living as a single mother. But the loneliness of being a single parent drove her towards spirituality. Church, followed by Yoga practice eventually brought her to India's Allahabad. In Allahabad she joined an Ashram for mental peace, learning Yoga side by side. Taty being a six-year-old at that time picked up Hindi and in a year's time was fluent in the Indian language. Once back in France, her mother didn't want her daughter to forget Hindi. There was also a selfish intent there. Her career as a Yoga teacher would have more authenticity if she had a Hindi speaking daughter at home. Then again if Taty had to continue her mother's profession, her expertise in Hindi would come in handy to prove her authenticity. Hence, she was put into Toulouse's only Indian school which taught Russian also as a second language.

So, when this Indo-French cultural organisation called up for French girls knowing Hindi and interested in India, Taty was thrilled to join them. But she soon realised that it was much more than just a cultural programme. Behind the guise of culture, an arms deal worth billions of dollars was being facilitated with the Indians. Most of the cultural programmes were hosted on behalf of arms dealers and were frequently adorned by top decision makers from the Indian defence.

It was after one of those cultural programmes that Taty was asked by one of her French organisers to escort an Indian defence official back to France and during his stay in Paris. She expectedly was stunned and refused. But what awaited her was a tough choice. A clear warning that if she did not oblige, what she would see once back home would be her mother's corpse. And if she did oblige what awaited her once back home would be a cheque of 1 Million Euro.

Taty thus lost her virginity to a fifty plus moron soon thereafter. And thus, was born a spy who could give Mata Hari a run for her money.

Chapter 58

Taty's credentials as an international spy were very easily traced by Mudgal. But what intrigued Mudgal was that how KK, whom 2i had used as a tool, had managed to outsmart them. Then again, the rendezvous between Taty and KK was staged by 2i. "What went wrong?" Mudgal, for the first time in his career, felt upstaged by a rival. But who was that rival? He could not wait to know.

Naturally the doubt was leading him to Taty, on her loyalties. Whether she was being a double agent. But after having discovered about KK's adventures in St. Petersburg, Mudgal had consulted his office. It was then he was told that it was his own people who arranged such a trap for KK, whom they were expecting to be a loose mouth. So, before the enemy caught hold of this fool, they decided to wrap him up. His people vouched for the loyalty of Taty and told Mudgal that it was better they looked for other loop holes which must have caused the damage. But Mudgal had this gut feeling, that something was amiss with Taty. And usually Mudgal trusted his guts more than logic.

For the next few weeks, half a dozen 2i sleuths were deputed to find more about Taty. And it did bear fruits. What specifically drew interest for Mudgal was Taty's blogs, obviously with a pseudonym. The blog was standing out with her numerous articles on anti-nuclear activism. Her connections with an Indian NGO fighting nuclear power plants stood out conspicuously. She was extremely critical of Russian and eastern European companies that were into nuclear equipment. Her ire for these companies stemmed from the strong belief that it was one of these companies which caused the Chernobyll disaster which took her father from her and pushed her mother into a lifelong melancholy. In short, she had a hatred for the word Nuclear.

Mudgal though good at connecting the dots, this time was fumbling. Not because he could not, but because what it suggested was something horrendous for his country. It was clear to him that Taty in fact had an axe to grind against nuclear submarines, and this could have prompted her to make inroads into Waveproof. Since KK was fully wrapped by 2i, it was clear that money should have come to Shikhar through Taty. Taty was a regular traveller to UK as per her travel blogs, and really enjoyed tiding over the English Channel. The scale of her bank transactions in UK pointed to a bigger role for her in international espionage.

But two things kept bothering Mudgal. One was the identity of whoever was sponsoring Taty, if at all she was behind what happened with the Stingrays. A young girl's revenge alone could not be the reason for a break-in into one of the world's best defence forces. The money and will-power were somebody else's and Taty was only a conduit for that real mastermind.

The second thing that gave butterflies in his stomach was the thought that if Taty's vengeance for nuclear installations was true and if there was a powerful and rich source behind her, then something more nefarious was in store. And it was in fact pointing towards that, once he could trace where all Taty had travelled in India. For once, Mudgal prayed to God that his gut feeling should go wrong.

Chapter 59

Taty's itineraries in India showed her repeatedly visiting a famous Indian nuclear power plant. And what disturbed Mudgal further was that this plant was also made with a Russian collaboration. If she had any ugly plans for this nuclear establishment then that would be a death knell for the crores of Indians residing in the near vicinity. Unlike Japan's Fukushima or Ukraine's Chernobyl, any place in India was densely populated. A nuclear disaster like any one of these would result in a fatality affecting the population in huge numbers. Mudgal was holding a lighted cigarette, totally lost in thoughts, without smoking it. Later on, he lighted another one adding the earlier one to the huge heap of cigarette butts. He was really tensed.

Taty at this time was enjoying holidays with her Italian boyfriend in Turkey. Istanbul's famous Sophia Mosque had this couple moving around soaking in the finest details. Taty being a die-hard fan of famous American author Dan Brown was re-living the experience of his iconic novel – Inferno. It was ironical that Taty had a striking resemblance with the thinking of the novel's main female character Sienna Brooks. It was as if the ghost of Sienna had got into her body.

Taty's boyfriend Frank had an Indian mother. His maternal family was the royals of a western Indian state. Later on, the family fully got into national politics and were now part of the ruling elite. But their obsession with power made it impossible for them to sit at the opposition for a long time. The rise of a mercurial leader in India, the Lioness, had made life miserable for these power-hungry parasites. Lioness was a no-nonsense person when it came to defection. She hated people with double loyalties and always kept them at an arm's length. Their main revenue while in power was through the lucrative commissions in defence deals. But with the ascent of the Lioness that abundant source of money had stopped. And with her popularity increasing day by day, they were desperate to do anything to bring the downfall of this popular icon.

Frank, being the agent for a reputed Italian defence manufacturer, was badly hit because of the Lioness. So, during one of those hot sessions during their yearly trip to Swiss Alps, Frank mooted this problem to his mate. Taty then told him about her hatred for nuclear installations whether it were submarines, power plants or bombs. She also briefed him about what she was planning to spoil the Indo-Russian fleet of new generation nuclear submarines.

It was then that it dawned on Frank what Taty could do to dethrone the Lioness. And two years later, now when they were going through the Sophia Mosque, reliving the Dan Brown thriller, Frank was a content man. What he mooted as an idea, his sweetheart was on the brink of making it happen.

Chapter 60

Puri was one of the four pillars of the Hindu religion.

The Adi Shankaracharya, in his short life of 32 years, travelled all the way from Kaladi in the southern state of Kerala, to the four corners of India to revitalise Hindu religion. He established four *Shankara Peeths* or religious centres to propagate Hinduism in its current format. In the process, he managed to drive out the influences of Buddhism and Jainism from India. If Puri was to propagate the *Rig Veda*, similar centre in Sringeri in the south was to propagate the *Yajur Veda*. Dwarka in the west propagated the *Sama Veda* and Jyotirmath in Uttarakhand spread the message of the *Atharva Veda*.

Very near to Puri was the Konark sun temple. This temple had this legend of holding the abode of sun's powers. It was true that once in a year sun came to such a position that the sanctum sanctorum of the temple got illuminated with its rays on sunrise. May be the Indian government had taken cognisance of the sun's romance with this place, when they decided to locate the most ambitious of Indian nuclear power projects here. The Indo-Russian joint venture was the result of the excellent Indo-Russian relations at that time.

And it did take off within five years, giving the whole eastern region a flood of 6000 MW of power. It was widely believed that the hitherto defunct development of the east will be put back into the track once this power plant would be operational. The secessionism which was showing its ugly face mainly because of the imbalance in development would therefore die a natural death. This was the political calculation of the Lioness.

The plant had six units of 1000 MW each. The design was based on natural uranium, thereby reducing the dependence on import. The reactors were well protected with the best of security. Being a non-IAEA audited plant, government took all the steps to keep away the plant's details from foreigners. Unless for the maintenance or repair of running equipment, no foreigner could ever dream of even coming close to the gate. Even the service personnel, if they were foreigners, would be audited by the Department of Atomic Energy before they could be given permission to go inside.

Agent X was the recruit designated to carry out that operation. Inside the reactor dome at a level of 6 metres was the Calandria. Calandria is the womb in which the nuclear reaction takes place. It is a drum like structure kept horizontal, flanked on both sides with perforated end plates. Through these perforations are the tubes inserted which would have the fuel bundles stacked inside. On both sides of Calandria are fuel handling machines. These machines have robotic arms which would take out the end covers of the tubes and then feed fuel bundles inside. On the other end of the tube, another robotic arm would similarly take out the spent fuel bundles. These robotic arms are controlled by a fully automated machine which runs on a software. The loading pattern is pre-fixed and the amount of fuel bundles are stored accordingly. Since it is a high radiation area, no human interface is allowed. Restricted human interface is, however, allowed during breakdowns or routine maintenance shutdowns.

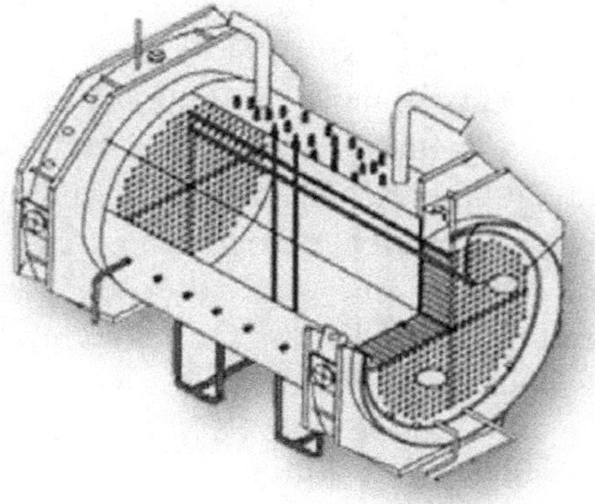

The software manufacturer was the same firm that manufactured the software 'Camaraderie' for the formation of the Stingrays. Agent X had managed a visiting card that claimed that he was the service engineer of this firm. He had convinced the power plant operator to be the successor of the previous service engineer who as per agent X had to leave the organisation. For authentication he was carrying a letter from the firm in Finnish, duly translated and notarised in Finland. For Taty, arranging such things was a piece of cake compared to the tougher things she had done.

It was easy for Agent X to access the fuel feeding machine during a routine shut down for maintenance. But even during routine maintenance, the shut-down access areas could be accessed only for a limited time. The radiation levels are measured and as per the millisieverts (msv) level, the duration of a single person's accessibility is decided. Expectedly, Taty had a solution; she advised Agent X to conduct a training session beforehand for the software updates required. This update would be carried out by the operator's plant engineers. And Agent X would visit the area only for 15 minutes, just to check the veracity.

Chapter 61

The shutdown date soon arrived and Agent X was there at the site to carry out his operation. As per the plan, the training session was carried out a week prior to the shutdown. The software was updated by the plant engineers who entered the area, in turns, for very short durations, as radiation levels were more than 1 msv. Soon it was Agent X's turn to check the update.

The feed rate of fuel bundles was set in the software as per the designed rate of reaction. Once it is set, the machine keeps on loading and removing on this rate unless changed by the operating engineers in the control room. But what the latest update had done was to change the calibration of the weighing device of the fuel bundles. This weighing device is in-built to the arms of the machine. Once the weight is measured near to the set value, then only it is fed to the tubes. By changing the calibration, the actual amount of fuel that goes into the tube would be much greater than the set weight in the system. Thus, the bundles were getting doubled without the operators knowing it. This was because the unloading arm's weight calibration was not changed at all. Hence the unloading rate remained the same, though the loading rate was double.

If left unattended, the reaction rate would double. The heavy water quantity was set so that it could absorb only a specific rate of neutron formation. But now, with double the neutron formation, it would fail to absorb half the neutrons it was supposed to absorb to keep the reaction rate as per design. Cadmium control rods are inserted from the top perforations of the Calandria to absorb the excess neutrons, in case the heavy water fails. But for these rods to be fully inserted, it would require 18-20 seconds to traverse the full length of about 7 metres. During this time, heat dissipation through the primary water would be too deficient to control the heat build-up.

The ensuing result would be an exponential heat build-up like it happened in Chernobyl, that is, a 1000 MW reactor unit would generate a heat of 33 GW in a span of a couple of minutes. Before a manual intervention could rescue the case, the immense heat built-up would create an explosion, releasing a nuclear crowd. The severe heat would kill all in the near vicinity. And the nuclear cloud which would travel towards the land due to the incoming wind from Bay of Bengal, would spell a disaster for nearly 3 million people in the twin cities of Cuttack-Bhubhaneshwar.

The public anger and the democratic mayhem that would be triggered thereafter would definitely throw the Lioness out of power. The country otherwise would be led into civil unrest. The president would have no choice but to dissolve the government and throw the country into an interim election. Public ire would ensure the defeat of the Lioness thereby bringing Frank's maternal family to power. The plans were all perfect and everything was indeed going through as planned by Taty and Frank.

Chapter 62

The only entry to the reactor was a three-door entrance wherein the first and third doors were never opened at the same time. The air inside the dome had chances of having radiation content. So, as a safety measure, the doors were designed in such a way that the air inside the dome never got exposed to the air outside. The ventilation air of the air conditioner was purged at a height of 150 metres through a chimney to avoid human interaction.

"You can fool all the people some of the time, and some of the people all the time, but you cannot fool all the people all the time." Agent X, who was coming out, was greeted by the security guard with this famous quote of Abraham Lincoln that was portrayed prominently on the security room just outside this three door gate. "Yes Bala, I'm talking to you." The guard turned back after having read the lines to Agent X.

Bala froze for that moment. If that voice had created a flutter in his heart, that face made it stop for a moment. Commander Abdul Latif's charisma was something that could never be hidden behind the uniform of a security guard. "Don't try to be smart my boy, it's the world's third largest defence force you have 'taken panga' (locked horns) with", Latif shrugged at Bala who was looking out to flee as a knee jerk reaction.

Three armed military men came out of a military jeep parked behind a huge banyan tree. The banyan tree was supposed to be a tree that exhales oxygen even during the night, thus justifying its presence outside a nuclear reactor. He was taken into the jeep by the armed soldiers and then it followed that Toyota Land Cruiser which was already on its way to an unknown destination. The jeep though puffed and panned to keep pace with the Japanese marvel. Latif in his trademark compassionate style slowed down every now and then to accommodate the lesser machine.

Bala was having the tensest moments of his life, blindfolded and a gun barrel pointed at the nape of his neck at all times. Latif on the other hand was looking at the fading domes of the reactor in his rear-view mirror, smiling at himself. He knew the best minds from Bengaluru, sent by Lingam, were setting the things right there. "Fingering us Indians on anything related to computers, do not waste time foreigners." Commander Latif was smiling, proud at this thought in his mind.

Chapter 63

Bay of Bengal towards the coast of Puri had some of the most beautiful beaches. The water was always blue, the waves always strong. Foreigners and a few Indians who had a love for surfing made the best of these beaches. They could surf without the fear of sharks chopping off their body parts.

The military had just hired the guest house of a prominent Indian company facing the sea near to the Puri beach. It was hardly a 100 metre walk to the waters from that bungalow. The sprawling British era bungalow was the holiday home of British generals residing in the then Indian capital Kolkata. But the bungalow has been renovated inside to accommodate the best of modern luxuries. But from outside it still looked like the fabled Dracula Castle in the famed Brom Stoker Novel Dracula.

The two serpents draped over the Globe adorned the gates, as if indicating to Bala, what a venomous creature he had become off late and was now a threat to humanity. The serenity of the blue seas could never settle his disturbed thoughts. For that matter, water in that ocean would have been insufficient to quench the fire in his mind. Doing a crime was like riding a motorbike without a helmet. You regret it only when you have a fall (obviously if you are still alive to regret it).

Mudgal was out there in the balcony, his Marlboro white cigarette burning fast due to the heavy sea wind. The Sun was just rising, the silhouettes of fishing boats out for an early catch making a picturesque sight. The first few rays of dawn fell on Mudgal's bald head and reflected. Latif was just entering with his cup of steaming filter coffee and this reflection reminded him of a famous Malayalam verse, "Maanavendra Vilangunnu, Chandraneppol Nin Thala (Dear majesty, your head shines like a full moon)."

"What are you smiling for? I know you guys have gone one up with this victory" – Mudgal jibed at Latif. "I was smiling at the brilliance remitted by your grey cells", Latif replied, gesturing at the reflection. Comradeship between two of India's best officers were visible. In fact, Latif was carrying one more cup, this time tea, in his other hand for Mudgal.

"What made this boy do this?" – Mudgal opened the topic signalling that both of them felt sorry for Bala. He will be soon arrested for treason, an offence which would haunt his family for generations. Reminiscent of the famous Amitabh Bachchan movie in which a little boy's hand was tattooed "Mera baap chor hai" (My father is a thief), Bala would have his coming generations being taunted for being a traitor.

Mudgal had just arrived by the early morning flight from Delhi. He was curious to know what had transpired here while he was busy hunting in France.

Chapter 64

"I had a doubt on Bala from the very beginning. Even when we caught Shikhar red-handed, I had this feeling of something was left behind. After browsing through all of Shikhar's email communication and browsing history, I knew one thing. Shikhar was good at computers for only one thing", Latif paused for a moment before continuing, "and that was to see pornography." Latif had contempt on his face when he said this.

"He was not somebody who could carry out this software stuff, which is more of a technically savvy job. Though I had my colleagues indirectly grilling Bala for over a month in Mumbai, I had strict instructions not to get physical with that young man. We had no evidences, not even serious doubts. I could not have used third degree methods on somebody just based on my gut feeling. If it had proved wrong, I would have wasted a young man's life." Latif followed Mudgal to the room as it was getting hot. The water level in the sea was also receding as a low tide was slowly setting up.

Breakfast was ready and reminiscent to the sun, freshly made bull's eye was awaiting them. Mudgal chose for *Upma and Sheera*, whereas Latif gorged on the eggs and toast. Typical of the guest house culture, fruit juice and fruit salad were served without even asking whether it needs to be served. But as expectedly seldom anyone told no to fruits and juices.

After breakfast, both of them went on a stroll to the receding waters looking for the famous turtles of the region. Olive Ridley sea turtles migrate in huge numbers from the beginning of November, every year, for mating and nesting along the coast of Odisha. Gahirmatha coast has the annual nesting figure between one hundred to five hundred thousand, each year. There had been decline in the population of these turtles in the recent past due to mass mortality.

They settled on a rock, Mudgal with a bottle of beer and Latif with his favourite, Sula White Wine. The caretaker brought in *Onion Pakodas* and *French Fries* to munch on.

"We had put some of our men to check on Bala's family back in Hyderabad. There we came to know about a five bedroom villa being booked in the name of his mother. Going by even the lowest market rate, that villa would cost not less than Rs 5 crores. If it had been in the name of his in-laws we would not have doubted. His in-laws were the erstwhile royals from Karnataka, his being a love marriage. Buttresses my belief that love is blind, that lady being beautiful and rich, and Bala just the opposite." Latif continued having sipped on the wine and enjoying the heavenly taste.

"We have been secretly checking his banking transactions but nothing was indicative of this huge amount. But what gave him away was his Red Santro car. We had put a red alert on this car in Mumbai, tracking all its movements. There was a particular mutton shop he used to go travelling sixteen kilometres all the way to Mahim from Andheri. Driving sixteen kilometres in Mumbai to buy mutton. And this used to happen every second Saturday in a month. Some of our informers in Mahim gave a clear tip, that mutton shop is a centre of hawala transaction." Sun was getting over their head

and Latif indicated to move back to the Bungalow wanting to complete his talk. "Let us go to that canopy there, let us see whether we can snack on some local fish." Mudgal was already high, more than the beer, because of the discussion.

Latif frowned at the suggestion but Mudgal convinced him by saying, "Come on Officer, we do not meet every now and then."

Chapter 65

Bala's phones were tapped, his internet activities were under surveillance, his office was bugged and his car was continuously followed. There were four times he had visited a theatre in South Mumbai to see French plays. Twice he was accompanied by Shikhar. The sleuths who sneaked in the play had seen both of them interacting with a blonde lady in Hindi.

But nothing suspicious could be ascertained against the French lady as Bala and Shikhar were seen speaking to many other members of the crew. In fact, those plays were socialising sessions as well, since that community was a close knit one. Other than a French lady speaking Hindi, cops could not find anything that was weird or out of place.

But Bala's activities thereafter got the cops on their heels. The frequency of his trips to the mutton shop had increased. Hackers had traced a letter he had submitted to the operators of the power plant as a proof for being the new service engineer for a software company. Bala being very much on the pay rolls of Waveproof, it was not understandable. That made the officers check up with the power plant on the details of this software company and where that software was being used. The details which came back from the plant sent the investigators into a tizzy.

Mudgal at that time was given a very short brief and he had put Latif across to Lingam. Mudgal also briefed the prime minster on the looming threat to the nuclear power plant. The whole machinery was put on high alert and a planned shutdown taken so that the perpetrators could be caught red handed. And it did indeed work out.

Bala had sent a confirmatory message from inside the reactor room to an unknown recipient. The email was sent from his personal address. The recipient's address was a generic address customercare@ruspberry.com wherein the company name was Raspberry and not Ruspberry. The mistake was understood as intentional, as the hackers later could not find a bouncing message in Bala's inbox. Normally if the email goes to an incorrect address because of a spelling mistake it bounces back. And since there is no word like Ruspberry, it was indeed expected to bounce back. The message was a routine service completion mail, but it had a small footnote in French that translated to 'Turtle eggs will hatch soon.' The footnote was well camouflaged with a quote by Charles De Galle, so an unauthorized recipient could never decipher it. But the cyber cell of a well-advanced country like India could decipher even tougher cryptic messages.

The cyber cell quickly got into action to find out where the email was accessed. The mail was accessed at two places, one in Istanbul, Turkey and the other in Mumbai, India.

Chapter 66

Bala was expected to spill the beans. They tried the good cop bad cop strategy first, but to no avail. Then they offered to make him a prosecutor's witness, if he could cooperate with the investigators. But he kept on saying he did it for money and had no clue who was behind it. It seemed he did not have even a clue about what the software 'Camaraderie' had been intended for in the Stingrays. Soon, the caretakers of the bungalow were taken out by the private company's administration team for an emergency internal meeting.

Then much against Latif's will, Mudgal made the cops do some third-degree questioning. The secluded bungalow was witnessing a professional interrogation for the first time. The cries of the young man reverberated against the walls of the bungalow. The sea was disturbed and a high tide was forming fast. Winds were blowing at abnormal speed. It was nearing sunset and the birds were hurrying home, sensing the sudden change in climate. All of a sudden, the sky was overcast and it started raining. The Bay of Bengal started showing its true colours.

Latif was a disturbed man. He was somehow developing a deep sympathy for the young captive. Money for a struggling middle-class man was always alluring. And in Bala's case, he had to prove a point to his in-laws and a dominating wife. He was fed up of living in perennial ignominy of being the poor husband of a rich woman. As a salaried man, it would never be possible for him to stand up on his own against the might of his in-laws.

Latif was not able to take it anymore, he rushed to Mr Mudgal and requested him to stop this interrogation. He said, "Give me a week's time and all your resources, I will bring the kingpins to you. Please leave that young man. He truly may not be knowing much. He is just a small fry."

"God only will save you if you don't deliver, I'm telling you," Mudgal's face was red when he called off the torture. "I will wait for one more week, on eighth day I will personally shoot that traitor bastard." Mudgal was visibly shaken at the interference and rushed to his room.

There was an eerie silence that evening. Caretakers came late in the evening and dinner was laid by ten in the night. Mudgal did not turn up for dinner. Latif limited his dinner to a handful of fruits and retired to his room.

What awaited them next morning was Bala's dead body.

Chapter 67

Mudgal, who was furious last night, was tense after hearing about the death in their custody. He wanted the post-mortem to be done quickly so that the reason for death could be known. A special task force from the Odissa police arrived at the bungalow to take care of the body and carry out the post-mortem.

Latif and Mudgal were not in talking terms at all. Latif was convinced that the third-degree torture was what killed Bala. But Mudgal would not accept it; he was sure that postmortem results would clear the air between them.

Meanwhile, a missing person complaint was filed at the Colaba police station by Waveproof, on behalf of Bala's worried family. There were some press reports in Mumbai and Hyderabad newspapers about the missing person and the rumours that were fast spreading across. Waveproof maintained that he was not reporting for duty since a couple of days, without notice. They said they were contemplating disciplinary action after he returned. But his missing report came to them as a surprise.

The post-mortem was done at Bhubaneshwar Government Medical College Hospital. The results showed potassium cyanide as the cause of death. This came as a shock to both Mudgal and Latif. They had done a thorough check on Bala after having caught him, to avoid any chances of suicide. It was routine procedure for the cops. Since this was an international espionage and sabotage case, extra care was taken. Moreover, the people who were interrogating him as well as the caretakers of the guest house were subjected to a thorough examination before they were let inside the bungalow.

There was no way that cyanide could have been either consumed by Bala himself or given by anyone around him. Both the officers were flabbergasted and did not know what to do.

It was at this juncture that the forensic experts who were examining the post-mortem report as well as the body came out with some important information. Bala's stomach had traces of gelatin that was indicative of him having swallowed a capsule. But the cops were damn sure that he had not taken any such capsule in the last 48 hours. And it was highly unlikely that the gelatin remained intact inside the stomach for more than 48 hours. That ruled out the possibility of Bala having consumed this capsule before he was caught.

Chapter 68

Far away in Istanbul, Taty and Frank were getting tense. It had been five days since the stipulated plant shutdown was over but the plant had not been operational. Once the plant became operational, it was not going to take more than a couple of days for the explosion to take place. The rest of the huge ransom would come to her only after that. She was worried about the fortune that would make her a multimillionaire in no time. What an ascent for a once hapless child who struggled to grow up under a single mother.

For Frank, the business was about to start. Like him there were many arms dealers who would like to see the back of Lioness. They collectively were ready to pump in more money to manipulate public opinion to swing the national elections in the favour of opposition parties. For that they had already drawn up plans with business analytics and psephology companies to manipulate social media. Most of the social media companies were ready to share their database for money. It was an easy game and a nuclear explosion will be the right trigger to change opinions.

Mudgal and Latif, after a day's mourning, quickly swung into action. Bala's death acted as a catalyst for their enthusiasm and resolve. Like Latif, Mudgal also off late had developed a posthumous sympathy for Bala, now knowing that he must have fallen into the lure of money. But the real culprits were still in hiding. Mudgal wanted to catch hold of Taty at any cost. He knew only she could bring the nation's enemy into light. He was sure that it was Taty who must have accessed Bala's mail in Turkey.

He had already put an alert to Interpol and the Indian embassy in Turkey to influence Turkish government to nab her. Since there was no extradition treaty between India and Turkey, it was looking difficult. And Istanbul being a tourist haven, Turkish government did not want to take any chances which would affect its reputation of being tourism friendly. And there was no ample proof with him as demanded by Interpol. International arrests could not be made based just on suspicions.

It was in a flurry that it dawned on Mudgal to check the room that Bala had stayed in at the nuclear power station. The police found the usual toiletries, sprays and a bottle of Seven Seas cod liver oil capsules. A normal police squad would not have seen anything suspicious with those, but not the country's premier intelligence agency.

The Seven Seas capsules were examined, and the forensic lab revelation was surprising. Each of these capsules were supposed to be filled with cod liver oil. But the oil was smartly sucked out through a small perforation. And through that perforation tiny cyanide capsules were inserted. The perforations were thereafter closed with wax. Then each of these capsules were neatly wrapped with a transparent thin plastic and sealed with an instant liquid adhesive. So, to the naked eye, the capsules looked no different than the original cod liver oil capsules. And for somebody popping it in the mouth just before sleep with the lights off had no chance at all to find any fault.

The killer must have observed Bala's habits very closely and would have done this to kill him slowly. The culprit had planned it so meticulously that a plastic layer over gelatin capsules would take more than 48 hours to melt inside the stomach. It was obvious that the Seven Seas bottle had been replaced by the person who must have given the final orders to Bala.

Since Bala was being closely monitored it was easy to find out who all visited him at his residence. And there was a person who not only visited Bala, but also dropped him to the airport in a rented car. And his name was Fernando Coutinho, yes, the trader from Hyderabad. All fingers pointed at Fernando. He must have changed the bottle either at Bala's residence or while dropping him in the car. But was he the big fish Mudgal was waiting for?

Chapter 69

Fernando was picked up by the Mumbai airport authorities based on a red alert received from the Home Ministry. Mumbai, after being subjected to so many terror attacks, was always ready to tackle any aggression. He was caught from inside a flight to London that was taxiing to the runway. The flight was brought back to the boarding bay and he was picked up by the commandoes.

Fernando had a tourist visa, and London being London, in all probability, he was never going to come back. It was understood later that the gift for killing Bala and may be for many more services rendered to derail India was to get transferred to his Swiss bank account that was openly accessible from London.

It was not only Fernando, but Taty also who was back to France by now, who was getting restless because there was no news coming from India on a nuclear mishap. But her confusion was soon cleared when the French secret agents whisked away her away from the Charles De Galle airport in Paris. The Indo-French relations were the best after Lioness took over, and France was eyeing India as a major market for its high technology products in the field of railways, power, shipping and defence. The high market potential India offered prompted them to nab Taty and a trial in an international court was set up to offer quick justice. The email sent by Bala and received by her (which was earlier substantiated by the hotel authorities in

Istanbul) was proof enough to hold her as a suspect in a planned but foiled terror attack.

Indian authorities deputed by 2i were part of her interrogation process overseen by the friendly French secret service. To corroborate further, the facts and figures were cross-checked with what was revealed by Fernando. It was now clear that Taty and Fernando were just mercenaries, with somebody else calling the shots.

Chapter 70

For Waveproof, Bala's death was a shock. Ram was clearly upset since he lost a bright spark from his submarines team. Whether Shikhar or KK headed the division, Ram was happy as long as Bala was around. He always felt that Bala was his man since he always got his reporting without the knowledge of the division heads. Losing such a man to 'brain haemorrhage' and that too at such a young age was sad, really sad. He felt bad for Bala's wife and daughter.

They were having the monthly review meeting chaired by Namy. Since the board meeting was due next week, this meeting had an added importance. The most critical issue was the project execution status of the new order of submarines, since it had attracted lot of media attention. Though both of them were annoyed at the ministry's arrogance in holding Shikhar at Delhi for no reason, that particular issue was never discussed.

The discussion was halfway through when the door was suddenly pushed open. Both Ram and Namy were visibly perturbed at the sudden disturbance. They had specifically asked the secretary not to allow anyone till meeting gets over. When they saw Latif entering the room, both of them squealed in a blend of surprise, displeasure and anxiety.

"Yes officer, what a surprise! What brings you here?" Ram was not able to contain his discontent and forgot the etiquette. As a tit for tat, Latif replied "Indian armed forces don't need anyone's permission to enter anywhere if it is in national interest" Latif was miffed at Ram's arrogance and showed Ram his place. After all a military man is any day above a civilian.

The tense air was irritating Namy and she apologised to Latif. "Please come officer. Nothing in Waveproof supersedes national interest. Our doors are open all the time for India's defence forces." That cooled Latif a bit, he settled on a chair and pulled out his laptop.

"I take heed of what you just said Madam, and hence taking the liberty of coming in without permission" the quick entry of Mudgal was received with a shock. The Chief of 2i visiting Waveproof uninvited, sent jitters down the spine of both Namy and Ram. Ram's face was devoid of arrogance and was pale due to not having any idea of what was going on.

"We are sorry for having gate crashed like this, but I was curious to see your premises, given what Latif had described to me. Pardon me for the intrusion." Mudgal's justification but did not cut much ice since it was evident that there was more than what met the eye.

Latif turned his laptop screen and asked them if they recognised the face on the screen. It was that of Taty. Both of them expressed their ignorance, but Mudgal just smiled. Then they questioned them about Bala, for obviously they said he was not on duty, and that too he was absconding. Hence, they could not give any details of his whereabouts and how he met with this untimely death.

"Are you sure you do not know that foreign girl?" Latif, apparently due to his dislike for Ram, was looking at Namy only. Namy hid her annoyance as she said, "I already told you I have never seen ...." Before she could complete her sentence, Pritam Pal Singh and Manpreet Sodhi (Shakespeare and

Shelley) shoved two tired people into the room. With them came in three armed commandoes too.

"But this person is very sure that you know her, Madam." Pritam pushed Fernando on to the table and shouted "*Bol saale*, Fernando (Tell, Fernando you scoundrel)". Namy Ferrao's face was white; it seemed like the blood had suddenly drained out from her face.

Chapter 71

"Manes of a Queen"
Manes reminiscent of a queen
Shines amidst the sunshine
Smiles light up a million hearts
Glance that pales a thousand Watts
Desire is thy name
Delight in your fame
Stroll like a wave
Still like a dove
Nod your beauty is a craft
God sure is a man of art

Latif stared at this poem that was prominently displayed in Jeremy Ferrao's office. A poem that Jeremy wrote for his love decades back. The lines were written in the memory of their days together in college. Those lines spoke of the dreams they had for each other.

But some religions frown upon inter-faith marriages. They insist that if one marries outside of their faith, then either he/ she is considered to be out of this faith, or he/she should get the other person to this faith. They can't remain as husbandwife following two different faiths. So, religions tell us whom to marry and how to live. Latif was miffed at this thought.

The Lioness was peeved and lost all respect for Jeremy when he proposed that she change her religion to his. She regretted that she was loving a religious bigot all those days.

But the fact was that Jeremy came from a small, close knit community and did not want to sever ties with them. His affinity to his community, and not his religion in particular, made him ask her to convert.

The Lioness decided to remain a spinster thereafter, having lost respect for romance and probably for all men. Jeremy fell in the groove of community and religion, settling for a girl from his own kindred. Being from the small sized community, Namy knew about this erstwhile romance and for whom that poem was written for.

Each time she saw this poem her hatred and resolve to annihilate Lioness quadrupled. Each time a politician heaped praise on her community for being very nice people and how they rose from refugees to rich, her blood boiled that even after more than a millennium, people here still considered them as refugees.

That refugee tag was getting onto her nerves and she started hating this land. A land that welcomed her forefathers when they had no other place to go. A land that accepted everything from invaders to travellers as its own and allowed to flourish in its soil. A land that celebrated both atheism and theism as part of same belief. A land that never invaded any other land not because they did not have the strength, but they believed in coexistence. A land that always prayed for the well-being of the whole world. A land in which some people believe eating even roots of a plant is hurting it, leave alone animals and fish. Above all a land that taught the world the power of ahimsa.

Latif, as he stared at the poem, had tears in his eyes.

Chapter 72

Latif came out of his thoughts when he heard the rumbles of an incoming helicopter. He rushed out to see the lady officers of 2i holding Namy and taking her towards the helicopter. Mudgal was waiting for Latif and nodded at him, gesturing that he board the flying machine. Latif was eager to hear from Mudgal what all Namy had confessed.

Mudgal narrated the story while having a cup of hot Irish coffee sitting towards the rear of the helicopter which was on its way to Delhi. A few weeks after Waveproof had received the trial order for submarines a rival company from the west approached her with a huge deal. If she could sabotage the software to keep the submarine fleet together, then she would be paid US $ 60 Million. That was about Rs 400 Crores. This was a strategy adopted by western companies to bring a bad name to their competitor companies from the poor countries of Eastern Europe. After having created a cartel between themselves, these rich companies then charge a ransom from hapless customers who would be forced to abandon eastern European products for the perceived inferior quality.

Namy accepted the deal and the company put across Taty as the contact person. Taty, as a woman in this espionage circuit, was simultaneously used by 2i to honey trap KK. 2i never had the idea that they were using a market resource easily available for anyone, and they did not care about it much at that time since it was a routine honey trap these agencies set to keep control of some loose character individuals.

Fernando was the man chosen by Namy to execute this, since he was perceived as an outside man by the world. Though in reality, Fernando was an escort to Namy wherever she went on private tours. Much before Jeremy was bedridden, Fernando had sensed the difference in personalities among the two. Namy, an outgoing and effervescent lady, was not a match for a workaholic and intellectual husband. After a day's hard work, Jeremy used to unwind by writing poetry and prose. Namy knew very well who was still inspiring Jeremy to write and she just hated it. Fernando, with his charm, filled the gap for her.

Fernando had this knack of judging people and he chose scapegoats like Shikhar and Bala to carry out the plan. He purposefully kept away KK from this, knowing that he was a drunkard and loose mouth. But he used KK very cleverly to trap Bala. KK never had a clue of what Fernando is doing with Bala. Shikhar also was offered a huge compensation, which he opted through Dubai. The malware software was delivered by Taty during one of those French plays held in Mumbai. The butcher in Mahim was a conduit arranged by Fernando for Taty to dispense the cash needed to carry out the plan.

The main remuneration was to be deposited in a Swiss bank account that belonged to Namy. But before that, another deal came to her as a testimony of her efficiency in successfully completing the first. The deal was so lucrative that she could not resist. Then again, once a thief always a thief.

Chapter 73

US$ 150 Million was offered by the same set of western manufacturers to sabotage the nuclear power plant. But Namy had second thoughts about it. She had plans to settle abroad with Fernando once the money for first deal was realised. With Ram at the helm she would have no difficulty in steering the company from abroad. Jeremy was to be finished off with a high dosage of pain killers. It was easy since Jeremy was injecting pain killers on his own because of his perennial illness. It would appear he injected a higher dose by mistake.

But what again drew her close to this second deal, was Frank's family in India. That family and Namy's family were close family friends and Namy was particularly close to the matriarch in that family. So, when she approached her for doing something that could change her political fortunes, Namy could not say no to her.

Once she accepted the deal, the lobbyists changed their stance and said even the money for the first deal would be paid only after the execution of the second. Though she felt cheated, her vengeance for the Lioness prevailed and she accepted the deal.

This time Shikhar was kept in the dark. Bala was the one chosen for execution and Fernando drew up the plans with clinical precision. Raspberry documents were forged and Bala was introduced as their service representative. The original Raspberry representative was injured by Fernando's men in a bike accident and he was hospitalised so that he would not be a hindrance to carry out the plan. The malware software to change the fuel loads was delivered by Taty to Namy and Fernando during their leisure trip to Singapore.

Bala had to be finished off since he could have become a nuisance afterwards. Given the magnitude of the calamity, Fernando was sure that one day the cops would reach out to Bala. He wanted to plug the gap. And that day he changed the Seven Seas bottle while Bala was freshening up in the bathroom.

Chapter 74

The arrest of a high-profile person like Namy could not be kept under the carpet for long. The press sniffed it somehow, and the whole media went gaga about a story that put the best of fiction novels to shame.

The blame of treason against one of its community members took all of them by surprise. The community being so nice, they right away came out with a decision to oust Namy from their community. Moreover, after having taking concurrence from Jeremy, the community decided to make Waveproof a public limited company with no private owners. The family's shares were donated to a public charitable trust taking care of child malnutrition and women welfare. The community members went a step further and created a trust for the welfare of defence widows with an enormous corpus. One wealthy businesswoman donated her fifteen storeyed building to provide accommodation to disabled soldiers.

A detailed report of the episode was presented to the prime minister. Mudgal could see her eyes getting wet when the photograph of Jeremy's office and the poem displayed there was shown to her. "Will he be bed-ridden forever?" Mudgal's answer to her query was only a meaningful smile. Did she blush for a moment?

Chapter 75

"Fact is stranger than fiction." Commander Latif turned and smiled at his newly wed wife in their honeymoon suite in Maldives. He had just finished reading the newspaper story of an unconditional Chinese pull-out from the Andaman. As a goodwill gesture to the timely Indian covert help, they lifted the embargo on Indian made cars. That made a big difference to India's electric car industry which boasted of the largest manufacturing base in the world. They would pip the Chinese competitors by sheer quality and price. China off late had become highly costly when it came to labour. The only way China could resist the Indian manufacturers was either by imposing high import duties or by putting an embargo citing security reasons. They had chosen the latter. But now, Indian manufacturers had access to a US$ 600 Billion market. The Chinese Premier's words for the Indian Prime Minister hit the headlines world over. "We have lived peacefully for more than 6000 years, and most part of it as world's two most prosperous nations until foreign powers looted us. Let us stay together always and continue as world's two superpowers making this world a better place to live."

The Indian tricolour was again flying high in Andaman, with all its magnanimity. Commander Latif stood up and saluted the newspaper picture bearing the flag.

His beautiful Russian wife, Maria Semenova Latif, stood there with an inquisitive face. Reading her mind, he took the

Gallantry award from his table and showed the inscription on it to her. It read "Satyameva Jayate" (Truth Alone Triumphs).

www.ingramcontent.com/pod-product-compliance
Lightning Source LLC
Chambersburg PA
CBHW062136160726
48282CB00027B/845

* 9 7 8 9 3 5 3 4 6 1 9 0 4 *